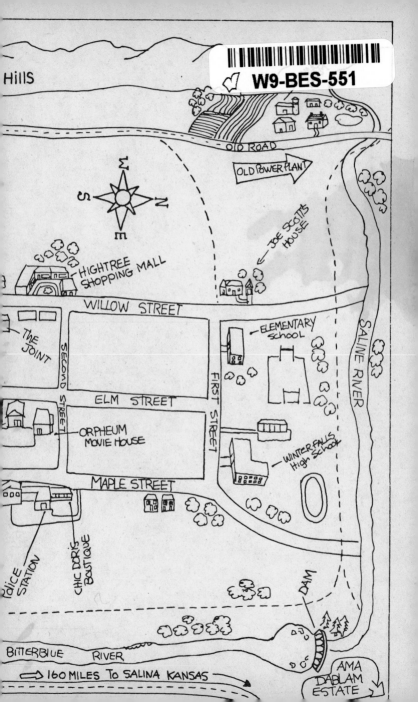

The Secret
of the
Third Eye

A Grand Lama from the Orient returns to Winter Falls, planning to use his newly developed mental powers to help his neighbors. But a scheming businessman has other ideas for using and *abusing* the lama's powers.

Observant sleuth, Jenny Dean, gets wind of the businessman's plot and tries to stop him in his tracks. But even Jenny, to be saved from danger, must rely on THE SECRET OF THE THIRD EYE.

THE JENNY DEAN SCIENCE FICTION
MYSTERY SERIES

The Secret of the Third Eye

By Dale Carlson

Illustrated by
Suzanne Richardson

Cover illustration by
Gino D'Achille

Publishers • GROSSET & DUNLAP • New York

For my daughter Hannah
who is my Jenny and my joy

ISBN: 0-448-19003-6.
Library of Congress Catalog Card Number: 83-47880.
Text copyright © 1983 by Dale Carlson.
Illustrations copyright © 1983 by Grosset & Dunlap.
All rights reserved.
Published simultaneously in Canada.
Printed in the United States of America.

Contents

CHAPTER 1

First Warning

By nightfall, Jenny Dean would be lost.

Right now, though, it was still a golden November afternoon, and she and Mike Ward had just climbed on their bikes. They were going camping, just north of Winter Falls, on the grounds of the old and mysterious Ama Dablam Estate.

"Keep an eye on her, Mike," said Dr. Howard, Jenny's father and one of the best veterinarians in Kansas. "Even in the woods, she'll find problems to solve."

Dr. Howard gazed adoringly at his daughter, not only at the dark, bright, intelligent eyes and the mop of short, blond hair, but at the small, sturdy self who was afraid of almost nothing and curious about almost everything.

Mike, as crazy about Jenny as her father, gave Jenny a protective hug and nodded. "I'll keep an eye on her, Dr. Howard."

Dr. Gwen, Winter Falls' leading psychologist and Jenny's mother, exchanged a secret smile with her daughter. They both knew how splendidly capable Jenny was of not only taking care of herself, but everyone else in sight.

"The Ama Dablam Estate has been deserted for years, hasn't it?" asked Jenny. "What can happen with no one around in the middle of nowhere?"

"Nothing, I hope," said Mike. "You've just finished helping Captain Fisher solve *The Mystery of The Hidden Trap*. It's time for a rest."

They were off, then, under the endless blue of the Kansas sky.

They cut over to the left from Willow Street to Old Road which skirted downtown Winter Falls. They rode north past the downtown section, and then cut east across Winter Falls' three main streets, Willow, Elm, and Maple, to the road along Bitterblue River on the east of town.

It was a habit of Jenny's to map out wherever she went, to keep track of any new details along the way. When she and Mike got to the river road, they followed it northeast, up toward the old Ama Dablam Estate. They would camp at its edge, near Bitterblue River Falls.

"Hey," Jenny called out, five miles into their

journey. "Could you slow those long legs of yours down a little?"

They were both athletes, both on Winter Falls' tennis team. Mike was not only the coach, he was also the team's star player. Too often, he used their outings to strengthen and train Jenny's already fast legs.

"Okay, I hear you," Mike called back. "I forgot this was supposed to be a day of rest for you."

Jenny smiled across at the tall, well muscled young man with the black, curly hair and the golden eyes. She loved the way he looked.

They had been friends since the second grade. Last year something else, something special had happened, and now Jenny was Mike's girl as well. They expected to have a future together. But that was someday. Right now, there was fun to have and life to live.

They raced for the wooden bridge over Bitterblue River Falls. They planned to camp on the other side, in the Forest of Ama Dablam.

"I'll pitch your tent as well as mine," said Mike, "if you'll go for firewood."

"It's a deal," said Jenny.

She felt fine, even after biking and picnicking and

exploring all day. Her hiking boots and her navy, down jacket were warm against the growing evening chill. Jenny felt free and happy as she started off into the Forest of Ama Dablam. That's what the thickly overgrown wooded part of the Ama Dablam Estate was called.

Even though Jenny had a good knife, it wasn't easy hacking through the vines and brambles that clung to the old, thick trees. But in half an hour, Jenny had cut her way far in from the sound of the waterfall cascading into the Bitterblue River—and even farther from the sound of Mike's voice calling out to cheer her on every few minutes.

"Leave it to me to pick a place like Ama Dablam for a rest," she grumbled to herself.

Jenny didn't know why exactly, but at the back of her neck she already felt the strange chill she had learned to connect with the uneasiness of the unknown.

"Silly goose," she said. "Pull yourself together. You've seen too many movies, that's all. Now, pay attention to firewood."

By nightfall, Jenny had an armful of firewood.

By nightfall, Jenny had spent her curiosity for the day and was ready to return to Mike, a warm fire, campfire food, and her sleeping bag tucked under her own small tent.

Only by nightfall, Jenny was aware that, as always, her warning signals were true, and that there was something strange going on in this tangled, old forest.

To begin with, Jenny was lost.

CHAPTER 2

An Unforgettable Sight

She kept on going through the darkness, glad for moments here and there when the clouds parted to let through the silvery light of a three-quarter moon.

Normally Jenny had a superb sense of direction. Usually she wasn't thrown even if she wasn't quite certain where she was for a while. But there was something mysterious about this brambled, vine-hung forest. Something mystical about the whole Ama Dablam Estate suggested feelings beyond the normal, beyond the ordinary physical world.

As Jenny went on cutting her way through more and more undergrowth, hoping to arrive somewhere soon, anywhere soon, anywhere at all, she tried to remember the story of Ama Dablam.

She knew the estate was named after Mt. Ama Dablam, one of the high Himalayan snow peaks near Mt. Everest, the highest of all mountains on earth. These high places that bordered Tibet and Nepal were called the Roof of the World. And they were the home of the most metaphysical kind of Buddhism. In these high places, in the monasteries and lamaseries of Tibet, secret powers could still be learned.

Jenny went on cutting, cutting and remembering.

An old man, born more than a hundred years ago right here in Kansas, had made a lot of money in Kansas winter wheat and cattle, Kansas corn, salt, and chemicals, Kansas oil and dairy cows—but what he wanted most, he said, he couldn't find in Kansas. What he wanted, he said, was the power to find out the secrets of the universe.

Jenny waited for the moonlight to shine through again to get her bearings. The moonlight shone again, but she was still lost.

"Just keep cutting," she said aloud. She had long ago learned to talk to herself, just one friend to another, she called it, as a way of keeping off the things that go bump in the night.

What was the old man's name? She went on trying to remember the story of Ama Dablam to keep her mind occupied. It was one thing to feel lost. It was another feeling altogether, wondering if you were ever going to find *yourself* any time soon.

Edward Plum was the old man's name. He had worked hard all his life, readying himself for the day when he would go to Tibet. He planned to study the mystical metaphysical powers that he hoped would help him foretell the future, understand the nature of the human mind, and see into the secrets of the stars.

He bought this vast, 10,000 acre estate. On it he built an exact replica of the Tibetan lamasery he had read about and loved most. Hidden behind the many-roofed, massive, sloping walls were one hundred rooms. He filled the rooms with beautiful golden statues, paintings, carvings of Buddha and old gods, and with texts and scriptures of old teachings.

And then, Jenny remembered, old Edward Plum died, died before he ever got to study in Tibet at all, much less even visit his beloved lamasery.

In his will, it was said, he left everything to his one surviving grandson—on one condition. His grandson, Edward Plum III, was to fulfill his grandfather's dream. He was to go to Tibet and do all his grandfather would have done if he had not died so soon.

Edward Plum III, in short, was to become a special kind of Tibetan lama, not just a monk, but a master, a guru, a Grand Lama of inner vision, a Lord Abbot with the power of the Third Eye.

Jenny remembered, some years back, hearing that Edward Plum III was a gentle boy, agreeable to whatever was expected of him. He had gone, it was said, as his grandfather expected, to the lamasery in Tibet.

Jenny wondered if Edward had ever returned to Winter Falls or was ever going to. Then she wondered if she could return to Winter Falls or was ever going to.

It was at this point, in the middle of this haunting forest, that she wanted to forget about Ama Dablam, about Tibetan mysteries, about Edward Plum and his grandson. Instead she wanted to think about some pleasant and familiar things—like the breakfast she had shared with her parents and Mike earlier that morning. They had been in the warm, sunny kitchen. The kid goat from her father's examining room had been wandering under foot. There had been waffles for breakfast.

But right now, both the night and the forest seemed to be growing thicker and darker and more ominous.

"Something doesn't feel right," Jenny muttered to herself, just to hear the sound of a human voice.

"Keep cutting," she said, "just keep cutting and putting one foot in front of the other. Remember some more things about home."

The Dean house on Willow Street was wonderful, Jenny always thought, even when she wasn't in trouble. Her mother had an office in the front of the house where she saw patients privately. She also worked at the clinic two days a week. In the back of the house in a special wing, Dr. Howard had examination rooms and a laboratory for the small animals he treated there, when he wasn't making rounds of the outlying farms.

Jenny loved living in a home where people and animals came for help and usually left feeling better. Since someday Jenny wanted to be a psychologist like her mother, and Mike wanted to be a veterinarian like Dr. Howard, they both hoped to have a home just like the one Jenny grew up in.

What Jenny wondered right now was whether she would ever see her own home again, much less have a future one.

"I've got to get out of here," Jenny said aloud. "If only I knew how."

She plunged ahead through yet another thicket. When she gathered her strength for another plunge, she felt herself breaking through at last. When the moonlight shone through the clouds again, though, it wasn't shining on a familiar sight.

Instead what Jenny could see clearly in the silvery

moonshine was the Ama Dablam mansion. It rose against the pale moon like a Tibetan lamasery growing out of a rocky cliff. Its many sloping walls, flat roofs, and tapering windows soared high into the night sky like the faraway mountains themselves.

It was a magical sight. Jenny stood as if struck motionless.

Strange words went through her mind, words that described the powers of the mind. *Clairvoyance*, the power to see what ordinary eyes couldn't, the past, the future; *telepathy*, the power to communicate to another mind without words; *telekinesis*, the power to move objects, send tables and forks flying around the room; *levitation*, the power to raise one's own body into the air; *healing*, the power to know what sickness a human body had and to know how to heal that sickness; and *meditation*, the most interesting word of all to Jenny, the power to get beyond the self to be at one with the whole universe . . . these words came to Jenny now as she stood rooted in the rose garden of Ama Dablam.

Her English teacher at Winter Falls High School, Miss Casey, was always interested in the parts of the mind that weren't merely the intellect. "She would be fascinated now," said Jenny. "I would be fascinated, too, if I were back in the middle of a classroom discussion. It's a little less fascinating—maybe even scary—standing at the foot of a Tibetan lamasery all alone in the moonlight wondering if your mind and your body are going to be able to stick together in one piece.''

A few more words occurred to Jenny besides levitation and other psychic powers.

She heard herself say words like, "Move. First one foot, then the other, Jennifer Dean. Right, left, right. Mind the rosebush. Ouch, that was a thorn. Good, lawn. Find the path, the driveway, road, anything that points away from here. Fine, that feels right under the foot. It's a gravel path. Keep going. Say goodbye now.''

The moon went behind the clouds again. Jenny kept her feet going however, until suddenly there was no more gravel, until suddenly she felt the bramble and vines of forest undergrowth once more.

Was she headed for the way out of the forest at last? Or was there something more to fear?

It was a short-lived debate.

She cut and plunged through a major chunk of undergrowth. And as the moonlight broke through again, so did Jenny. She found herself staring up once again at the great, massive walls of Ama Dablam. How had she gotten back here?

This time, though, she saw a light in one of the narrow, tapered windows at the side of the lamasery. Jenny picked her way out of the rose garden and crossed the lawn to look up.

As she stood not far from the dimly lit window, she saw a figure appear. He seemed to be carrying a candle, or perhaps he had already placed it on the windowsill. The face of the man, it seemed to be a man because of the shaved head, was rather yellowish, the eyes narrow, heavy-lidded, and nearly closed.

The whole evening was already so bizarre. Jenny felt that a force had drawn her to Dablam. She felt that she could not get away from the lamasery. Jenny wanted to flee but she was unable to do so.

Just as she began to back away, determined to again try that gravel path, something happened that once more rooted Jenny to the spot.

The strange face gazed down on her from the narrow window. Then what Jenny saw next, she knew she would never recover from. The face closed its ordinary two eyes, and in the center of its forehead, opened a third. In the dark night, the Third Eye gleamed a deep, ruby-red.

CHAPTER 3

Drawn Again

"You saw *what*? He was *where*?"

Laurie Harper's stage whisper rang across the school auditorium, as she and Jenny bent over the flat they were painting for the next school play. Laurie came from one of Winter Falls' most prominent families. She was also, as Jenny described her, "tall, thin, beautiful, sensible, captain of the basketball team, and an A student, as well as Jenny's best friend" which, as Jenny sometimes added, "made Laurie merciful as well." "And tired," Laurie would add fondly.

She shuddered again at Jenny's story.

"*What* did Jenny see? *Where*?" Claire Richmond, their school's best artist, and Karen Porter, their best designer, came over to hear the details of Jenny's latest escapade.

Most of Jenny Dean's escapades turned into Winter Falls' most exciting police cases sooner or later, and everyone wanted to hear the story she had been telling Laurie Harper.

By the age of sixteen, Jenny had developed a capacity to notice things and a habit of making mental lists of things most people never noticed at all. Her parents, her friends, and especially Detective Captain Ray Fisher of Winter Falls' Police Department had often made use of Jenny's extraordinary talent for observation and for her almost total recall.

"I beg all your pardons," came the deep, theatrical tones of Joe Scott from the stage at the other end of the auditorium. "The junior class Christmas pageant is less than six weeks away. As your director and leading man, may I ask that you pay as much attention to Charles Dickens' *A Christmas Carol* as you're paying to Jennifer Dean's *A Night in the Spooky Forest*?"

Joe Scott was Mike's best friend. He was handsome, black, popular president of the Student Council, and liked being all three. He was also an accomplished and an almost-professional actor and he was currently directing the junior class play.

"If, of course, anybody's interested," said Joe. But he too came over to hear the details, particularly since when Jenny and Mike needed extra help, Joe's judo and friendship were often called upon.

"I need you now," said Jenny, "or at least to-morrow, I need you, Joe."

She retold the whole story of her and Mike's camping expedition, about how she went looking for wood, got lost, and ended up at Ama Dablam staring up at a strange, sad, yellowish face in one of its narrow windows. She said nothing, however, about the Third Eye.

"So, if you were lost, how did you get back?" Laurie asked.

"I tried the gravel road again, and it worked," said Jenny. "It led me to a path that wound around some, but then took me right back to Bitterblue River Falls where Mike was waiting for me."

"And then you rode home instantly and called Captain Ray Fisher at once, right?" said Laurie, worried but without much hope. Jenny generally tried investigations out on her own before calling the police detective.

"Not exactly," said Jenny, patting her friend's hand.

"Well, what then, exactly?" said Laurie.

"Well, exactly what we did was camp out the way we planned and came home Sunday morning," said Jenny. "And exactly what I want to do now is go back there."

"Mike and I will go with you," said Joe.

"I'm going, too," said Laurie. "This time if you get lost, you'll have a bodyguard."

"I'll make a deal with you," said Joe. "You finish Tiny Tim's fireplace flat today, and we'll all go back to the Ama Dablam Estate tomorrow right after school."

"The rest of the deal is, you stay late for tennis practice today," said Mike.

He had walked in with Alex Harte, Jenny's tennis doubles partner, just in time to hear the end of the conversation. "We've got a rematch with the Dodgetown team next week."

Mike wanted the Winter Falls' team to win the state championship and the new amateur trophy, the Hannah Bee Cup, sponsored by New Wave Sports Clothes. Winning would allow the team to travel and to compete nationally.

"It's the only way we're going to see the outside of Kansas any time soon," said Mike.

"No one's going to see the outside of this auditorium, never mind Kansas, unless we finish three flats and we rehearse the second act by four-thirty," said Joe.

"Tyrants," muttered Jenny. "Everywhere you go, tyrants."

"For one tyrant," answered Laurie sweetly, "I

direct your attention to Jenny Dean, organizer of a case investigation.''

"Funny," said Jenny. "Fu-unny."

The four got on their bikes at exactly two-fifteen, Tuesday afternoon after school. Mike had gotten the afternoon off from Flint's Hardware Store, Joe had canceled rehearsals, Laurie left someone else to coach basketball, and Jenny had put in a special call to Captain Fisher—just in case.

"Odd you should be heading up there," Captain Fisher had said on the phone. "The two hot flashes in Winter Falls today are, one, that Edward Plum's grandson is home from that lamasery in Tibet where he's been for the past five years."

"And two?" asked Jenny.

"The second hot flash is that Rolf Wind, the owner of that Electronic Videogame Arcade you guys all hang out at, has opened a back room for fortune-telling and such. He wants to capitalize on the new rage for oriental mystery in Winter Falls, he says," said Captain Fisher.

"What rage for oriental mystery?" Jenny wanted to know.

"That's what I asked," said the police captain. "He says he's going to start one."

Neither of them had ever had much use for Rolf Wind.

"Goody for him," said Jenny, ringing off.

The news about Rolf Wind's new oriental, fortune-telling room telegraphed a sensation of trouble from Jenny's middle to her brain. Maybe it's just personal dislike, thought Jenny, and she persuaded herself to stop thinking about Rolf Wind.

As the four rode through the sparkling, crisp November afternoon—past the red and gold drifting leaves of late fall elms, maples, oaks and the silvery birches that clustered along the roadside—Jenny thought of that incredible face. It was a sad face, withered, and so lonely. As for that gleaming, ruby-red Third Eye, between and just slightly above the eyebrows, Jenny decided she was glad she hadn't mentioned it to anyone. She just about decided it had been an illusion, and that probably she hadn't seen it at all.

"Tell me," said Mike, riding alongside Jenny. "Are we about to have the pleasure of your mental company any time soon? Or have you just brought along the body?"

"Sorry," said Jenny. "Have you been saying something to me?"

"I've been saying, Laurie's been saying, Joe's

been saying," Mike answered. "Only you have not been saying back."

"Was there something specific?" asked Jenny. "Or have you just been going on about isn't this terrific weather and aren't the leaves gorgeous?"

The four had their usual good time together during the two-hour ride. They left their bikes across the wooden bridge over the Bitterblue River Falls where Jenny and Mike had camped Saturday.

"So, now," said Joe Scott. "Which way to Ama Dablam?"

"We're on the estate already," said Jenny. "The house—house? It's more like a castle out of a far eastern fairy tale—is back in there, through the forest."

"Okay," said Mike. "You lead the way, Jen. We're right behind you."

"We'll *all* keep in mind, won't we, that Laurie has a date with Jason Kent to go to the movies tonight?" Laurie put in.

Jenny gave her friend a quick hug. Laurie joked when she felt cold, awkward, scared, or all three.

The four began to hack and cut their way through the vines and brambles. They still had more than an hour of daylight left, but it was darker under the overgrown forest than under the open sky.

Jenny worked harder than the others to get through.

"What's the drive?" asked Joe.

"You know Jenny," said Mike. "She thinks there's a poor soul back in there, and she can't resist nurturing everything she finds." Mike spoke fondly. He was proud of Jenny's caring about creatures and people and the fate of the world in general.

This time Jenny knew it was more. She did care, of course, about the sad face in the window. But she cared also about two things she hadn't mentioned— the feeling she hadn't been *just* lost, but had been *drawn* to Ama Dablam twice and, of course, the business about the eerie illusion of the opening of the Third Eye.

She was concentrating so hard on these things that she wasn't sure just when it was she found herself suddenly alone. Had the others dropped back? Jenny called out. There was no response. She called out again. The forest only echoed their names.

It was terribly clear. Whatever had gotten her lost the first time was operating again. It had separated her from her friends. It had done so purposely. She was alone. It was dark now, and she was alone.

She had also just broken through the last of the

undergrowth, and found herself in the rose garden again. All I have to do is look up, she thought.

"Come on, Jenny, look up," she said aloud.

But the loudness was really a whisper. She knew, when she looked up, exactly what she would find.

He was, of course, there, staring down at her from the narrow window. Once again he looked strangely sad. Once again, as his two normal eyes narrowed like the window, he opened the ruby-red, gleaming Third Eye.

CHAPTER 4

From High Places

Heavy, oak doors opened in the front wall before Jenny could take cover. Then there, in a shaft of light, looking straight at her, was a shadowy figure in long robes.

"Come with me, if you please." It was a monk. Although he sounded pleasant, his was no ordinary invitation. It was more like a command, that clearly was expected to be obeyed.

The monk gracefully beckoned Jenny through the large, carved doors and led her through the entrance hall to the room called the Great Hall. Then he bowed and quietly disappeared.

This was obviously the inner temple under the central pagoda-tiered roof outside. The four walls were pillar arcades, the lintels richly carved; and the walls were painted with beautiful frescoes. In the back of the Great Hall was a lavish Tibetan altar with its central golden Buddha gleaming softly by the light of hundreds of butter lamps.

In front of the altar, on an elevated throne carved like a flower, sat a man. He sat with his legs crossed in the lotus position with an ease Jenny hadn't yet attained in her own yoga classes. He was so still. The whole inner temple was so still! Jenny could feel herself relax and grow peaceful. She was strangely unafraid, even as she now recognized that yellowish face that had stared from the window.

She was hoping, however, that whoever he was, he would only open the usual number of eyes. She was also hoping that when the rather withered face came alive, it might tell her something of Edward Plum's grandson.

As Jenny waited quietly for whatever would happen next, she did a bit of arithmetic. Edward was eleven when he left, he had been gone five years, he would be exactly her same age now.

The impressive figure stirred on his flower throne. Jenny could see he was coming out of his state of meditation. She waited for him to speak.

"Hi, Jenny, remember me from the fifth grade?"

Jenny looked around to see if anyone else had entered the room. The voice was that of a fellow American in his teens.

"I'm up here. My name is Padme Lampo. It used to be Edward Plum."

There was no further question. The young man's voice came from that old man's face. Jenny moved closer to the lotus throne, but it was still hard to see him clearly in the dim glow of the butter lamp lights.

"That's right, come closer so we can talk," said the voice, so bright, so vital, so young that it was hard for Jenny to believe that it belonged to that face.

"I'll come closer, too. That way, we'll meet."

Jenny wasn't quite positive whether the figure jumped or floated down until he was beside her. It was such an odd motion. He was still in the lotus position when he arrived on top of a cushion at the foot of the altar. He gestured her to sit on an identical cushion nearby.

Padme Lampo's smile, or Edward Plum III's smile, or whoever's smile it was, was as full of white teeth and fun as anyone in Jenny's junior class. Maybe it was the shaven head. Maybe it was his saffron-yellow robes. Maybe it was the yellowish, weathered, narrow-eyed face, thin and sad despite the smile and the glad voice, that made him seem so old. What had they done to Edward Plum III? If this *was* Edward Plum III.

"Have no doubt it's I," said the young-old man.

Jenny jumped, to hear her thoughts answered.

"Of course I can hear your thoughts," said Padme Lampo. "That's among the easiest of my powers. I've been away studying at Sakia. Sakia is the name of the lamasery in Tibet near Mt. Ama Dablam where my grandfather, through his will, decreed me to go."

Jenny wanted to ask why he looked so much older than he ought to, why he looked so unhappy, but she said aloud instead, "What else have you learned?"

"Well, as you know," said Padme Lampo, "Tibetan Buddhism is based less on what Buddha actually taught than on many of the supernormal practices of India's Hindu yogis."

"I've been learning a little about the great teachers of India in my yoga class," said Jenny, "but I don't know too much yet."

"You sit well in the lotus position," said Padme Lampo.

"Thanks," said Jenny. "It's pretty comfortable after a while, that is, when my legs don't go to sleep. Go on—what would you like me to call you? Edward or Padme Lampo?"

"Padme Lampo, please. I've gotten used to my

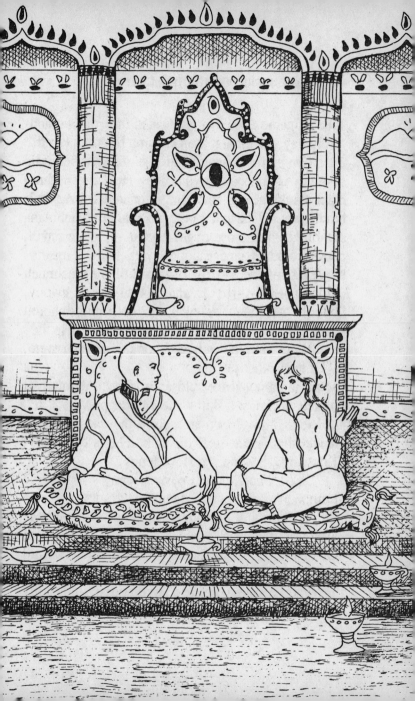

Tibetan name after so long," said the young man. "Anyway, the great man, Gautama Buddha, taught us to live in kindness and to leave our egos behind, so that we might have joyous lives. He taught us that right thinking, right action, right and loving behavior would lead to happiness. Buddha's teachings are simple, but those of the Hindu yogis are more complicated. Reincarnation, you know, means being reborn over and over again until one reaches a spiritual peace called nirvana. It's called *sanggye sa* in Tibet. Also there are all sorts of teachings about supernormal mental powers. These powers help the soul, the atman, to reach perfection or nirvana even faster than other powers."

Padme Lampo leaned closer to Jenny. "A lot of it is such nonsense. But some of the powers I've learned and developed are good—the ones, for instance, that let me heal the sick. That's to be my life's work, healing the sick, Jenny."

Padme Lampo looked up, over Jenny's shoulder. "Oh, thank you, Sonam. Jenny, have some *tsampa* and tea. You will like our Tibetan barley meal and milk dish, I hope."

Jenny turned to see the tall, robed monk who had first led her into the Great Hall bringing food. He left the tray and then pressing his hands together in salute, bowed and disappeared into the shadows.

"What are some of your other powers?" asked Jenny, sipping the hot tea with pleasure and finding the tsampa interesting.

"Well, there's the easy stuff like mind reading and fortune-telling."

"Easy?" said Jenny. "Easy?"

"It's no real trick to open one's mind to another's, or to crystal gaze or to read someone's color aura, or to send tables flying across the room," said Padme Lampo. "It's easy once you've been taught to see with the mind, not just the eyes and regular senses. After the inner eye, the eye of inner vision, the Third Eye has been opened, you are sensitive to everything. It's exhausting sometimes, actually. I also had to learn how to keep my Third Eye closed."

Jenny took a deep breath. "Then it was true, what I saw in the window. You actually opened a Third Eye."

"Some of us had a slight physical operation at the monastery to help our inner vision. Only those of us destined to be Lord Abbots or Grand Lamas had it. We are called reincarnations of our early great teachers, returned from sanggya sa to also help others through the cycle of suffering and rebirth to sanggye sa," said Padme Lampo. "The operation was a bit painful, but allows us to see into another's mind and future much better afterwards. Just a little hole is drilled. Then, to fill it in, since I was able to open the hole at will, a small ruby was inserted."

"Then you don't actually see with the Third Eye?" said Jenny.

"Not physically, no," said Padme Lampo.

"Mentally?"

Padme Lampo nodded. "All too often."

Jenny had an odd, quick thought. "Is that why you look so sad sometimes?"

"Ah, how sensitive you are," said the young man.

"I guess if I could read everybody's troubles every waking hour, I'd look quite sad myself," said Jenny. She finished the last of the Tibetan barley and milk dish without even thinking about it.

Padme Lampo clapped his hands, partly in pleasure, partly to bring Sonam back with more.

"And you also would like to know why I look so much older than my years?" Padme Lampo asked. "My training, the training of a Grand Lama who is someday to assume the responsibility of directing and caring for a great lamasery, is very hard physically as well as mentally."

"You mean," said Jenny, her laughter ringing through the temple hall, "they plumb wore you out."

Edward Plum III, the Padme Lampo lama, laughed aloud with her. Afterward, thought Jenny, he seemed just a little less aged.

"Show me one of your hard-earned powers," said Jenny. "Can you levitate?"

"Of course," said Padme Lampo. "Any sensitive, well-trained, well-disciplined body and mind can levitate. How do you think I arrived here from up there?"

"So that's why the motion was so odd," said Jenny. "You looked as if you were sort of floating."

"I wasn't floating at all," said Padme Lampo stiffly. "I simply remained still and let my mind move my body down to where you were."

"Oh," said Jenny. "Oh, my!"

"I can do better than that," said Padme Lampo.

Suddenly, the young-old man wasn't there. He simply wasn't there at all.

Then, Jenny heard his laughter. She looked up. There was Padme Lampo, still in his yoga lotus position, hovering up under the temple rafters.

Before she got used to that, he was gone again, first behind a delicately carved Tibetan god, then, finally, on his cushion in front of her once more.

"I haven't done that in years," said Padme Lampo, flushed with pleasure. "My teachers would have had a fit, knowing that I play with my power to materialize and dematerialize like that. I mean, it's positively forbidden to use the powers for anything but *good*. To use them for evil, to make money, or to even show off can give me anything from a bad headache to a loss of power altogether." He sighed happily. "My, that was fun, though."

Jenny found the grandson of Edward Plum such a mixture of youth and fun and an adult kind of religious holiness. She was absolutely fascinated.

One last question she didn't ask, but truly wanted to was—

"Why did I want you here, Jenny? Why did I use my mind power to draw you and only you to me?" Padme Lampo asked.

CHAPTER 5

Positive Powers

At that moment, two entrances to the Great Hall opened simultaneously. Through a curtain at the back, a young, lovely woman who looked like one of the bodhisattvas, the enlightened ones from the wall frescoes, came and stood by Padme Lampo's side. Through the heavy doors Jenny had first entered burst Mike, Joe, and Laurie, all of whom hurtled in relief toward Jenny.

"Welcome," said Padme Lampo. "Mike, you most certainly will make the top two tennis teams in the state competition. No, Laurie, you won't get back in time for your movie date with Jason, but your father will be home tonight from his business trip. Yes, Joe, even with fewer rehearsals, the Christmas play will be fine and next summer you will again be invited to join the summerstock group."

Jenny was grateful for so minimal a display of Padme Lampo's powers. Considering he could be floating among the rafters, or sending any of them flying across the room, just a little clairvoyance indicated a small effort in quiet good taste, Jenny thought.

"Thank you," Padme Lampo replied promptly, and winked at Jenny.

I don't want word about you to get around yet, she telegraphed back. *If even one of us gossips about you, even if it's just out of enthusiasm, you're going to be swamped by a lot of greedy people for everything from racetrack tips to Wall Street predictions.*

Now you know why I picked you, because I knew you would help me, because the colors in your aura told me you were among the good people. Jenny found herself hearing Padme Lampo's voice in her mind. He hadn't spoken a word out loud.

What she did hear aloud was, "I'd like you all to meet my friend, Caro. Caro has the art of healing and teaches me a lot of things. Also, she is from Tibet. I would have been lonely without her."

Caro smiled and bowed in greeting.

"She is the daughter of a great lama and a Russian princess," said the young Lord Abbot. "This explains her fair coloring and her great knowledge. It doesn't, of course, explain her affection for me, but I'm grateful for it nevertheless."

Mike was the first to recover his presence of mind. "First you disappeared in some uncanny way, Jenny. Then I had the odd feeling the rest of us didn't so much come here, as we were whisked here from the middle of the forest."

Mike looked around at the ornately carved temple hall, at the Tibetan Buddhist prayer banners and prayer wheels, at the frescoes of Buddha's life and the bodhisattvas, and at the yak butter lamps flickering near the altar. Then he breathed a happy sigh Jenny understood. They both loved the unusual, the varieties of human experience.

"Explanation?" asked Mike.

"How nice," said Padme Lampo. "Do sit down, Jenny's friends. Caro and Sonam will bring some fresh tea."

Tea, dried fruits, more tsampa, cheese, and some *chang*, a mild barley beer, soon appeared, carried in on trays. Everyone was hungry, and they all sat contentedly on their floor cushions to eat and talk.

"It's time to explain things to Mike," said Padme Lampo. As he smiled at them all, Jenny noticed two things. The young lama's face relaxed, not exactly enough to look youthful, but enough to appear less wizened, less ancient, less like a yellowed, old man. The second thing was that Padme Lampo kept his Third Eye closed. All that marked its place was a line that might simply have been another weathered seam in his forehead. Jenny wondered for a moment whether his inner vision, his ability to see into the heart of things, differed when the Eye was open or closed.

Then she began to pay attention to the explanation he was giving Mike, Joe, and Laurie.

"So you see, Tibetan Buddhism is a mixture of old gods and demons and reincarnation and complicated rituals from the Hindu as well as the teachings of Buddha. I myself simply follow the way of Buddha's teachings. He said that if people are kind and thoughtful and loving, they can be happy. Nirvana or heaven is already within us if we will only free ourselves from our own ego, our own willfulness, our Self.''

Padme Lampo sat very still in his yellow robes covered with the red robe of a Grand Lama. "I wanted to explain this to you, my new friends, because I don't want the healing of the sick—my powers of restoring health, to be confused with some religious nonsense. People do that, you know,'' he sighed. "It's why I'm better off not doing tricks. To say nothing of wasting energy.''

Jenny explained quickly what Padme Lampo meant about tricks.

Caro joined the conversation at that point, and with a musical ripple of laughter, said, "Padme Lampo used to get into such trouble at the monastery. Every time he learned a new power—levitation or dematerialization, or how to move an object telekinetically, he played with it. Then he slept for two days. Nobody could wake him. And his headaches!"

Padme Lampo nodded. "When any of the powers are misused, either just for fun or for material gain, Mike, the energy drains away and exhausts me and my head hurts. When any power is used for a good purpose, the feeling is one of being re-energized. I feel wonderful and replenished."

"So, I gather it was for a good purpose you telekinetized us all here," said Joe.

"What a word!" said Jenny. "But you're right, we're going to need a new language."

"And some new clothes," said Laurie, plucking and patting Caro's tunic blouse, shawl, and the flowing skirts of the Tibetan nun. "I love these, Caro."

"And some new judo moves," said Joe. "All this power is going to need protection."

"Thank you all," said Padme Lampo, gratefully.

"But what I need most, what I most need from you, is that you tell people I am here and that, if they are in pain, I wish to help."

It was in this touching and loving moment, though, that Jenny glanced up to the carved rafter beams. She had raised her eyes to hide her emotion. What she saw was a man's shadowy figure creeping stealthily toward the lotus throne and Padme Lampo!

CHAPTER 6

An Uninvited Artist

If Jenny's instinct was to nurture everything in sight, Mike's instinct was to protect everything. He had shinnied up one of the carved arcade columns, leaped across the roof beams, and collared the intruder almost before Jenny had finished the last note of her outraged yell.

"Got him!" Mike yelled back.

"Toss him!" said Joe, whose deep actor's tones needed no extra lung volume.

"Catch!" yelled Mike.

"Ready!" Joe yelled too, from excitement.

"Hey!" sounded an unknown voice, a protest from the intruder.

But his "hey" was a note in movement, uttered loudly in flight, on his way down from the temple roof beams to the temple floor. It was true Joe deadened his fall, but only just. All, including their new friend Caro, were annoyed at any threat to the gentle Padme Lampo.

Padme Lampo had sat perfectly still throughout the drama of a stranger, dressed all in black, being thrown through the Great Hall of his temple.

Now he simply asked in his quiet voice, "Who are you, sir?"

"Don't you know already?" Jenny asked.

"It's too exhausting to always read minds," said the young lama. He asked the man again, "Who are you, sir?"

The man pulled his dark jacket back into place and straightened himself stiffly from Mike and Joe's roughing up.

"My name is Mario. I work for Mr. Rolf Wind. I am an artist. We are decorating a room in the back of Mr. Wind's Electronic Arcade in the Tibetan manner," said the intruder.

"And you were sent to draw sketches?" said Laurie.

"That is correct," said Mario. He held out a small pocket sketchbook and a fistful of charcoal pencils to prove his point.

Jenny looked briefly at the sketches. Then she came forward and stood between the artist and Padme Lampo. Something about this man made her uncomfortable—either this man, his intentions, or his employer, Mr. Rolf Wind—she wasn't yet certain.

"Why break in?" she asked. "Why not ask permission?"

"I did," said Mario. "I asked him."

Mario pointed over Jenny's shoulder. Jenny turned to see at whom Mario pointed. It was Sonam, dark and forbidding in his tall, pointed hat and red robes. He was standing protectively over the seated Padme Lampo.

"He said no and meant no," Mario went on, "and there's something about him I didn't like to argue with."

"I understand," said Jenny.

"And if you know anything about Mr. Rolf Wind, you wouldn't want to argue with him, either," said Mario. "I had to bring back sketches."

"Well, Padme Lampo?" Mike asked.

Padme Lampo shivered a little.

"His aura, the lights around him, aren't a screaming orange-red, but they aren't very restful, either," said Padme Lampo. "His thoughts are self-serving, but not dangerous except indirectly. He also has a bad headache."

"Asking you questions isn't exactly like having a regular chat, is it?" said Laurie.

"It must exhaust you so," said Jenny, full of sympathy, "to see so much!"

"You understand!" said Padme Lampo gratefully.

"She sees too much herself sometimes," Mike explained, "and remembers it all—you know, she has one of those scientifically observant minds."

"The world is dying from lack of attention," said Padme Lampo. "It is good to pay attention."

"Right," said Jenny. "And while we *weren't* paying attention, guess who just disappeared?"

"It's all right, Mr. Lampo," said Joe, "we know where to find that artist."

"Mario won't get far," said Mike.

"We've got to go," said Jenny. "But before we leave, do you think you have enough protection here at Ama Dablam?"

Wordlessly, Sonam and Caro stepped forward on either side of their much loved Grand Lama, their young Lord Abbot.

Jenny nodded. "We'll be back. Please list the ways you want us to help tell others about you—by word of mouth, by written invitation, how many people you think you want to see in one day or one week. Shall I come back Thursday afternoon?"

Padme Lampo smiled in agreement. Even though he seemed old with his shaved head and great quiet wisdom, he looked like a sad and lonely boy when his new friends left.

"Did you see the sketches?" asked Captain Fisher.

Jenny and Mike had dropped by the police station on their way home. Captain Fisher was in his office, practicing some close-up magic with his new set of paper cups and furry red balls. Jenny sat on the edge of the captain's desk, watching his swift-moving hands.

She liked being near the tall, kind man. His warm eyes and lean, bony face were a study in contrasts. The captain could look positively satanic when angry—which he was constantly—at some of the political figures of Winter Falls. But he was a gentle man, and Jenny saw him as a kind of guardian angel of truth and compassion who kept law and order in Winter Falls. Captain Fisher did not carry a weapon. He always found a way to solve a case without violence.

"Well, did you manage to glimpse Mario's sketches, clever one?" repeated the captain.

"Yes, Captain," said Jenny.

"Is this conversation going to be like pulling teeth? Or are you going to give me a report soon?" said Captain Fisher. "Where is the furry red ball?"

"There," said Jenny.

"Really," said the captain stiffly.

"Is she right?" said Mike. "Your hands move too fast for me."

"She's right," said the captain. "As usual."

"The sketches have been bothering me," said Jenny. She got off the desk and went over to the captain's blackboard. She drew some things quickly, roughly, the way she did in her biology and biopsychology notebooks.

"Oh dear," said the captain. "Those sketches bother me, too."

"Anybody care to explain to those in the audience who are slower than others?" said Mike.

"The drawings," said Jenny, "were not just of frescoes and carved roof beams and Buddhas and altars and butter lamps and the rest of the Tibetan temple decor and architecture. They were also of Padme Lampo himself."

"Are you thinking what I'm thinking? Mr. Rolf Wind is planning to put something *else* in his new oriental room?" said Captain Fisher.

"Yes," said Jenny. "And why does that make me so nervous?"

CHAPTER 7

Guilty Lovers

"Jenny, it's ten o'clock at night. We've been going since seven-thirty this morning," said Mike.

"I know, I just want one quick look," said Jenny.

The two were outside the police station unlocking the wheels of their bikes.

Mike rolled helpless, beseeching eyes heavenward. "I love loving the smartest girl I ever met. I even love her urgent obsession to solve the world's problems every waking minute. But my, could I use a couple of grilled cheese sandwiches and a quart of banana ice cream, preferably in a sitting position."

Jenny was used to people teasing her about being smart and taking the world too seriously. Tonight, she was overtired. It made her feel odd, and different and a little lonely for a moment.

"Can't help it," said Jenny, her voice a bit cranky to hide the moment's emotion. "I have to go or I won't sleep, but you don't have to come with me.''

"Wrong," said Mike cheerfully. "The way you obsess over the world, I obsess over you. Wouldn't sleep a wink or eat a bite."

They telephoned their parents from the public telephone in front of the Chic Doris Boutique to say they'd be an hour late. Then they took off for the Electronic Arcade a block away on Elm Street.

The nine o'clock show at the Orpheum Movie Theater next door hadn't let out yet. There was, however, a crowd in the front room of the Arcade. The people playing *Donkey Kong*, *Pacman*, *Space Invaders*, and the other beeping, honking, bell-ringing games created enough of a diversion to hold Mr. Rolf Wind's attention. This allowed Jenny and Mike to slip down the alley between the movie theater and the arcade so they could see the upstairs back room.

It was easy. There was an old-fashioned fire escape. Mike leaped up onto the first platform and reached down for Jenny. His easy strength was most welcome. They were both peering in through the musty gray window in seconds.

"I was right!" Jenny exploded under her breath.

"About what?" said Mike.

"Look," said Jenny.

Mike looked through the window and saw what both expected to see. The back room of Mr. Wind's Arcade had been decorated to resemble—as closely as western paint, prefabricated columns, and the fabrics available in the middle of Kansas would allow—the exquisite Great Hall of the Tibetan temple at Ama Dablam. There were even frescoes, an altar to the Buddha, and a lotus throne.

"It's very nice," said Mike.

"Nice!" said Jenny. "Look what that man, that Rolf Wind, has done!"

"Jenny, if you're not going to tell me what's upsetting you, I'll never know," said Mike. "Myself, I'm not telepathic."

Jenny pointed again to something that was being worked on, being put together, in the center of the fake temple floor. The something was unfinished. Only a most observant eye could pick out this or that piece of fabric, this or that bit of wood, and know precisely what the unfinished object was going to look like.

"I knew it! He's making a replica not only of the temple, but of Padme Lampo himself," said Jenny angrily.

"I grant you it isn't a nice thing to duplicate

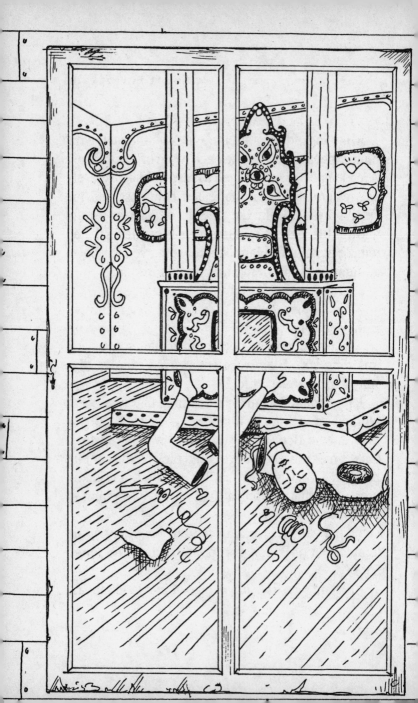

someone without permission," said Mike. "But it's hardly a crime, Jen. It isn't hurting anybody."

"Not yet," said Jenny. "Not yet, it isn't a crime. Not yet, it isn't hurting anybody. But it will, Mike. It will be a crime, and it will hurt a lot of people. I'm sure of it."

Suddenly a loud crack resounded in the dark. It sounded like a pistol shot. Then Jenny felt a distinct something whistle past her ears.

"Who is up there?" came a threatening voice, from a man carrying a whip.

Jenny flung her arms around Mike and kissed him, mussing up his hair a little in the process. When the flashlight found them, she called sweetly down.

"It's Jenny Dean and Mike Ward, Mr. Wind," she said, with a giggle Mike had never heard before and hoped never to hear again.

"Come down at once. There will be none of *that* love stuff on my premises." Rolf Wind's deep voice carried, and carried with authority. That voice and his whip had once enhanced his long career as a traveling circus barker. He used to call and con people into sideshows and big tops and into playing games of chance. His wasn't a kind voice. But it was quite loud and clear.

Rolf Wind was big and dark and threatening, as he stood there snapping his whip. Jenny and Mike came down at once and left, pretending guilt all the way.

"Clever!" said Mike as they rode off. "I told you I love loving a smart girl."

This time Jenny laughed.

Dr. Gwen spooned out Jenny's third bowl of black cherry jello and covered it for the third time with twice as much whipped cream. This came after two helpings of cheese lasagna, a vast salad, and several slices of Italian bread.

"I agree with you, there's going to be trouble," said Dr. Gwen. "Are you sure you've had enough dinner, dear? More pasta or salad, perhaps a plate or two, or the tablecloth?"

"I was hungry, Mom," said Jenny.

"Clearly, dear," said her mother.

"Anything that Rolf Wind is involved in seems shady, underhanded and something of a con to me," said Dr. Howard. "Never liked a man who could hit an animal, and I've seen him hit his German shepherd. That dog's going to turn on him one of these days. Besides that, he's been making a living taking children's chore money for the past couple of years with that arcade of his."

"And now he's working a scheme to take hard-earned money from adults, too," said Dr. Gwen, "to say nothing of putting nonsense into their heads."

"Poor Mom," said Jenny. "She spends every waking hour helping to deprogram people from their own nonsense so they can be free, and here's Mr. Wind trying to sell them some more fairy tales."

"I saw the new leaflets Mr. Wind has begun to circulate. They talk about his mysterious new oriental room built like a Tibetan temple with a Magical Computerized Fortune-Teller that tells real fortunes," said Dr. Howard. "Only five dollars, the leaflet says."

"Five dollars for a really dressy swindle, that leaflet ought to say," said Dr. Gwen.

"I don't like it," Jenny mumbled into her jello. "Aside from taking poor people's money for a pack of fake hopes, something else is wrong. I don't know exactly what, yet. But something else is wrong."

"You'll find it, dear," said Dr. Gwen. "If anybody is going to find out what's wrong, it'll be you." Dr. Gwen's voice drifted on in an airy way. "Other people's young daughters used to play hopscotch and have tea parties. Our daughter used to stand in the back yard wondering whether the wilderness or the lawn mower was going to take over Kansas. Other people's daughters used to play "I'll be the mommy, you be the daddy." Our daughter could spend four hours watching the ants organize and carry a crumb back to an anthill." Dr. Gwen's voice drifted on. "Other people's daughters wanted new skirts or jeans or a lipstick—"

"I want a Siamese cat," said Jenny.

"Our daughter," Dr. Gwen sang on, "wants a Siamese cat."

"Why?" said Dr. Howard.

"Padme Lampo is lonely. He needs a cat. Lama or no lama, he is also just a lonely boy away from the place he loves," said Jenny.

"And your feeling is that a pussycat is going to fix this?" said Dr. Gwen.

"Yes," said Jenny.

"There's more to it than that, isn't there?" said Dr. Howard.

"Yes," said Jenny.

CHAPTER 8

Caring Friends

Jenny spent Wednesday collecting opinions. There were three teachers at Winter Falls High School whose opinions Jenny valued. First she went to her English teacher, Miss Casey and to Mr. Altman, her history teacher.

They both agreed that the only odd thing about Padme Lampo was that in the West, people thought someone like Padme Lampo odd. "Psychology may be new in the West," they both said in different ways, "but in the East, yogis in India have been studying the nature of the mind for over two thousand years."

Then Jenny went to see Mr. Farley. She brought sandwiches and apples and tea bags to the biology lab so that they could have a long chat.

"How's my favorite biopsychology major?" said Mr. Farley.

Jenny described Padme Lampo and his healing powers, as Mr. Farley put hot water to boil over a bunsen burner.

"There's nothing freakish about your friend," said Mr. Farley. "He's been trained by experts, along with his own natural ESP talents. Most minds can be trained to use powers other than the intellect. We would be better off with more training in healing and less in fighting in the western part of the world," Mr. Farley added.

The lab telephone rang then.

"It's for you," said Mr. Farley.

Jenny listened for a few seconds and went pale.

"Who is that?" whispered Mr. Farley, concerned for his pupil.

"He hung up."

"What did he say that upset you so?" Mr. Farley asked.

"Jenny Dean, keep your nose in your own affairs, was what the man said," Jenny answered.

"Whoever it was must be keeping a pretty close watch over you to know exactly which schoolroom you were in," said Mr. Farley. "I mean, he'd practically have to be a cat climbing up this ivy to look in here."

Jenny had a sudden and total recall of Mario, the

artist who worked for Rolf Wind, climbing across the temple beams of Ama Dablam.

"Thanks for the observation," said Jenny. "Now I know whose voice that was, and I know who is really giving the warning."

The trouble with warnings was, all they did was make Jenny angry.

For her Thursday visit to Padme Lampo, Jenny had picked up a small, blue-eyed orphan Siamese cat from her father's lab.

She saw no reason not to go to Ama Dablam alone. Mike couldn't keep on taking afternoons off from his job at Flint's Hardware Store, and the rest of her friends had promised Joe Scott they would show up for rehearsal. Besides, they knew where she was likely to be. If anything happened to her, they would know where to look.

"Nothing is going to happen to me," said Jenny firmly to herself, strapping the cat box her father had left her onto her bike. Into the cat box went the Siamese, her flashlight, and camping knife.

By four o'clock, Jenny was over the wooden bridge at Bitterblue River Falls.

"See? Nothing is happening to me," Jenny said firmly to herself.

She parked her bike, picked up the cat box, and found the path that led to the gravel road. She removed the flashlight and knife from the box, leaving the kitty inside meowing loudly as only Siamese cats do.

"No wonder Siamese cats were used to scare off thieves in the temples of India and Tibet," said Jenny, "to say nothing of Siam and Cambodia and wherever else. I've never heard such yammering from any other kind of kitten."

The path was almost free of vines, but it was dark under the heavy overhang of elms and maples. Jenny touched the flashlight in her jacket pocket for company.

"Nothing is happening to me, absolutely nothing, and I'm fine," she kept saying to herself. Except just as she said it one last time, she heard a noise in the underbrush not far away.

She moved more quickly, muttering more quietly now, "See? Still fine. Coming right along now. Just fine."

The scraping noise in the underbrush followed her closely, not far from the path. It was perfectly clear the noise was traveling with her.

Her heart was pounding. So were her feet, running along until she came to the gravel path that led toward the lamasery.

Ahead were the massive, sloping walls, the pagoda roofs, and the heavily carved temple doors. As if on cue, they swung open. There was Caro, in an exquisite flaming orange *sari*, her scarves fluttering like prayer flags in welcome. Jenny flung dignity to the winds, raced past Caro, and on through to the Great Hall.

"I thought you might be lonely. I brought you a cat," said Jenny, nearly skidding to a halt in front of the lotus throne.

"I think you must be telepathic, too," said Padme Lampo.

He climbed down in normal fashion. He held out his arms, and Jenny opened the box. In a single, graceful motion, the Siamese cat leaped directly into the young lama's arms.

"How lovely, he likes you," said Jenny.

"He probably smells the fur on my robe from the temple cats at home," said Padme Lampo. "I was just sitting here this afternoon dreaming of the mountains, the way the sun gleams on the snowy peaks and on the backs of the mountain herds of yaks. I was missing the Sakia Lamasery and my friends, the Sherpa porters, who brought us supplies and stories of the outside world. I was missing the mountain air and mountain flowers and especially I was missing Milarepa, my own temple cat. Is this one really for me?''

"For you," said Jenny, glad to be giving pleasure.

"I shall call him Milarepa, too," said Padme Lampo. "Caro, have we some food, a dish for water? Will you ask Sonam for a small sandbox?"

Padme Lampo was clearly delighted with the small cat.

"I'm glad to see you," said Padme Lampo. "I need your counsel on the invitations."

From a pile of thick, creamy papers on the temple floor where the young lama had spent the afternoon laboriously hand-lettering each one, Padme Lampo handed one to Jenny.

It said:

> *We are pleased to announce the return of Padme Lampo, grandson to Edward Plum of Ama Dablam and now Grand Lama of Sakia Lamasery in Tibet, Asia. By appointment only, Diagnoses and Healings, Predictions and Observations by One Who Has the Power of The Third Eye.*

Jenny mentally compared this announcement to Rolf Wind's circular about his oriental room and his magical, computerized fortune-teller.

This was some week for Winter Falls! One prophet from the mysterious Far East, from the far places of the Himalayan Mountains, was about to freely share his joy and wisdom and power to heal. And another prophet, put together with nuts and bolts in the equally mysterious back room of the Electronic Arcade, was about to share its robotized hokum for profit.

"One's faith," Jenny said, "in the human race is about to be tested."

"I beg your pardon?" said Padme Lampo.

"I think your announcement is perfect," said Jenny instead.

Padme Lampo sighed, pleased.

Caro and Sonam came in, with a tray of food and tea for them, and a second tray of food and water and a sandbox for Milarepa, who was purring contentedly in Padme Lampo's arms.

Sonam remained dark and silent and unbending around Jenny, but Caro was as friendly as the last time.

The four sat down to tea. Jenny tried hard not to think of the darkness outside the gray-white walls of the lamasery, and who and what the darkness held.

Just for this moment, Jenny was safe.

CHAPTER 9

A Warning Voice

After tea, Caro accompanied Jenny along the gravel road, the length of the path, and even across the wooden bridge to the river road.

Jenny had mentioned the traveling noise that had followed her through the Ama Dablam forest. It followed them both now, but together they were unafraid.

"You're small, but you have a strong, sturdy body," said Caro, who approved of good physical condition as a part of good mental health.

"From you that's a compliment," said Jenny. She admired the looks of the tall, fit young woman and thanked her for her company. "See you tomorrow. I'll be just a bit later. I promised Mike a couple of hours on the court. We have a match soon, and my serve is off."

"You'll be in time for the first *Talk* tomorrow evening?" Caro asked.

They had decided to call Padme Lampo's sessions simply *Talks*. The young lama held Tibet's highest degrees, including the Lharampa Degree from Llasa's great monastery Deprung. He was adept at the Four Great Tantras and had a mastery of political science, medical science, astrology, and the psychic powers as well.

"But," Padme Lampo had said, "a lama is only a teacher, no matter how many degrees and powers. And a good teacher talks so that all may learn to help themselves and to not forever run to some guru or other. We will simply call our sessions together *Talks*."

"I wouldn't miss the *Talk*," said Jenny to Caro.

"If you'll be here at the bridge at quarter of seven, I'll bring you through the woods," said Caro. "It is Padme Lampo's wish that you be protected."

"I'll have Mike with me," said Jenny.

"Nevertheless," said Caro.

At quarter of seven, Jenny and Mike were at the bridge. Caro was waiting for them with three butter lamps, one for each of them. The yak butter burned brightly in the polished brass.

"What's that?" said Mike.

It was the same faint, thrashing sound that had followed Jenny twice before on the previous day.

"I'm being noticed," said Jenny dryly.

She felt Mike's gentle but firm arm around her shoulders.

"Stay close, Jen," he said.

"And both, behind me," said Caro.

The *Talk* had only just begun when the three entered the Great Hall of the Temple. Padme Lampo sat, not on his high lotus throne, but on a simple, wooden chair. He wore, not the robes of the Grand Lama he was, but a simple western shirt, slacks, and cardigan.

To Jenny, he looked very straight and small, sitting there so still. Despite his simplicity and his fragile size, Jenny felt his tremendous power, his tremendous intelligence and the energy with which Padme Lampo filled the room.

There were about twenty people from Winter Falls. As Jenny and Mike took their places on floor mats with the others, she saw Mr. Flint from the hardware store, Miss Doris who owned the boutique near the police station, Jenny's parents who had come earlier, Jack Ward and George, Captain Ray Fisher, of course, and Miss Casey, Mr. Altman, and Mr. Farley from school, among others.

Padme Lampo was speaking quietly.

"And so I have come back to Winter Falls, not as some silly guru, some purveyor of magic tricks, but

to share with you what I have learned so that you may in time learn to cure your own physical and psychological ills. Sadly, I am sure most of you will want to see a trick or two in order to believe me."

Padme Lampo was silent a moment. The lights from hundreds of butter lamps filled the dim heights and shadows of the huge temple hall.

"Dr. Gwen Dean, mother of Jennifer and wife to Dr. Howard Dean," said Padme Lampo. His voice was only slightly altered by his own instant self-induced state of consciousness. Caro had told Jenny it was a state of light self-hypnosis. It allowed him to pay the fullest attention to the vibrations he received, the way a radio receives sound waves at a certain frequency.

"Dr. Gwen, you are disturbed by one of your youngest patients. You feel the child's disturbance is physical, not psychological. You are correct. The child's pain is caused by a small brain tumor, perfectly benign and easily removable by surgery."

"I thought so," Jenny could hear her mother's firm, audible voice whisper to her father.

"Miss Doris," said Padme Lampo, "you need not have that abdominal operation, you know. You have simply an abrasion of the stomach wall. Take a long walk every day and some simple herbal drugs which you can obtain from any good drugstore.'' Padme Lampo then listed three everyday pharmaceuticals.

''For that painful stiffness, Mr. Farley, come to see Caro next week. A few simple adjustments of the vertebrae will take the pressure off the nerves, and massage will stimulate your blood and lymph glands. If you learn a few exact exercises and do them every day, I promise you complete relief from pain,'' Padme Lampo went on.

Rapidly, Padme Lampo touched on some problem of nearly everyone who had come to see him. For those who had medical problems, he diagnosed and prescribed treatment.

Other people, like Dr. Gwen, had personal or professional conflicts.

''Captain Fisher, you will soon experience something monumentally strange, something that will radically change your entire life, your entire perception of the universe,'' said Padme Lampo.

After half an hour, Padme Lampo came to himself. Caro, who always stayed with him to protect him in this nearly unconscious state, felt the temperature of his skin and seemed satisfied, Jenny noticed.

''I am tired now,'' said Padme Lampo. ''Today, I

have merely shown you how easy it is to pick up your thoughts, pain, and negative energy. Simple herbs and nontoxic, natural drugs, certain self-induced mental states, and some physical exercises can help to restore your health. We will have more *Talks*, public as this one; private when necessary. We will work together, to bring joy. Good night.''

They all rose to go.

Just as Padme Lampo himself was about to leave by the curtain behind the altar, he turned and half-raised his hand.

As if on cue, everybody fell silent.

Jenny wondered if this was the moment. Would the actual presence of the Third Eye and the glowing ruby in the center of Padme Lampo's forehead be revealed to all? Not so, not yet.

Padme Lampo still used only his two eyes, at least outwardly, to look at his visitors.

"There is something . . . evil in Winter Falls,'' came the strong voice of the young prophet.

The voice of the prophet wasn't joking. It added one more warning before the Grand Lama went behind the curtain.

"Jenny, my friend Jenny Dean, be careful!''

CHAPTER 10

The Know-all Robot

On Saturday morning, wrapped in turtleneck, bright-red lumber jacket, and long red underwear under her jeans, Jenny straddled a barnyard fence and strummed her guitar for the chickens.

Jenny often spent Saturday mornings making rounds with her father. While he treated the animals, she played to them. She hoped the music soothed them. It certainly soothed her.

They had already been to the Springer farm on Old Road north of town. They had just arrived at the Ward farm on Old Road south of downtown Winter Falls. Since his mother's death, Mike had helped his father manage the farm.

Jack Ward, his sons Mike and George, and Jenny's father had gone off through fields of winter wheat to check the cattle on the south pasture. Jenny was content to sit in the sparkling sunlight this fall morning, playing country-and-western music to the chickens and to Old Betsey. The old sow, nuzzling in her straw pen, was pregnant again.

"Her litter's due soon," said Jack Ward, when he and the others returned from the fields.

"I can see that," said Dr. Howard. "We'll give her a shot of Pituitrin to fight agalactia, so her milk comes in this time."

"Do you remember the last time she littered?" asked Mike. "I spent more time mixing cow's milk, eggs, and glucose and feeding the calves with baby bottles than I spent doing homework for two months."

"May have to again," said Dr. Howard. "Old Betsey's good at littering, but she's short on lactating and has been for years."

"You sound so cheerful," said Mike.

"I don't have to feed the piglets, do I?" said Dr. Howard, even more cheerfully.

"Let's go home now, Jenny. I'll make pancakes for breakfast."

Back in the Dean kitchen, the laughter, the familiar rituals, the murmuring stream of voices flowed to Jenny's contented ears with the reassurance that some things lasted and went on unchanged.

More and more, though, the sounds of her past, her early childhood, were interrupted by the technology of the new and present. The telephone rang. It was Captain Ray Fisher.

"Jenny to Captain, come in please," said Jenny, into the telephone.

"As you would say, fu-unny," said Captain Fisher, in a teasing voice.

"And you, what would you say?" said Jenny, teasing back.

"What are you and Mike doing tonight?" said the captain. "That's what I called to say—ask, I mean."

"It's the opening of Rolf Wind's Oriental Room with his Magical Computerized Fortune-Teller. I wouldn't miss it for the world."

"Good," said the captain. "The whole thing is making me nervous. I'm not sure why. I therefore want you to see it with me."

"We'll be there," said Jenny.

"See you later, then." The captain rang off.

The Electronic Arcade on downtown Elm Street was a mob scene by seven-thirty Saturday night. The videogame room was jammed and so was the sidewalk outside. Everybody was waiting for the Oriental Room, with its advertised Magical Computerized Fortune-Teller, to open its inner doors.

"At least there are going to be three of us here who have a hunch there's more to this whole operation of Mr. Wind's than just fun and games," said Jenny.

"Have you seen Captain Fisher yet?" said Mike. "With your mind click-clicking away like some weird inner meter looking for trouble, I'd feel a lot better with the fuzz around."

"*Fuzz!*" said Jenny. "You refer to my captain as the *fuzz!*"

Captain Fisher's lean, intelligent face appeared for an instant as the crowd parted.

"Fuzz indeed," said Jenny, with the captain's own dignity.

Mike laughed. He loved when Jenny acted like Queen Victoria.

"Come on," said Jenny, laughing at herself with him, "we'll meet the captain inside."

"Inside?" said Mike. "And just how do you propose to do that?—not the fire escape again?"

"Scrunch and follow," said Jenny.

She was better than a linebacker getting through crowds. In a few minutes, the two were inside, not far from the inner doors, and next to Captain Ray Fisher who stood lounging against the wall in his black turtleneck sweater and tweed jacket.

"He looks more like a movie star than a cop, don't you think?" Jenny said to Mike.

"He couldn't be more *divine*," said Mike, imitating Laurie Harper's imitation of Katharine Hepburn.

The few minutes laughter did all three of them good. For the next half hour, their responses were pretty grim. The doors of the inner room suddenly flung open.

"Welcome," said the deep tones of Rolf Wind, resounding over the crowded room until a hush fell on everyone. He raised his arms dramatically, as the practiced Svengali he was. As the people filed in, he managed to collect five dollars from each while conferring on all a sense of privilege besides.

Jenny watched his eyes glitter, and shivered slightly as she passed him going through the inner doors.

The Oriental Room Mario had designed was exquisite, a wonderful replica of the Great Hall at Ama Dablam. And at the back was an equally perfect— almost sinister it was so real looking—replica of Padme Lampo. The only discordant visual note in the room was the small set of lettered keys, like a typewriter, just below the lotus throne on which the robotized version of the young prophet sat.

Jenny heard Rolf Wind's theatrical tones explain.

"Simply type your question onto the keys. The question will appear on the small television screen above the keyboard for you to recheck. After a few moments reflection, the Grand Lama from Tibet will answer from his lotus throne. Beware, you may not get the answers you expect!"

"That covers all possible holes, doesn't it?" Jenny whispered to Mike and Captain Fisher.

But she was impressed. Mr. Rolf Wind was a man of many talents. Too bad all of them were dedicated to material gain. It was as if he wanted to get even for every penny everybody else had!

But the process Mr. Wind had put together was amazingly ingenious. Using a simple home computer programmed to respond to typed questions, he had rerouted the answering method through the robot's mouth and made it audible.

Jenny heard the first answer of the evening.

"Yes, John does love you."

She listened to more answers as they came in a thin, mechanical voice out of the mouth of the robotized Padme Lampo.

"Use chloride of gold on that skin ulcer . . . No, don't sell the store just yet, you will do better after the first of the year . . . Yes, you will have a child by a year from this Christmas . . . The palsy isn't a physical ailment, the child feels guilty about losing his school books and is shaking from fear of discovery . . . Yes, the Bitterblue River will flood that southeast field again this spring. Don't plant wheat as it will rot; you might try rice."

Jenny watched the incredulous faces around her. At first, many seemed just to view the whole business as fun, but as the hour wore on, many more seemed to change their minds.

"They're taking this seriously," said Jenny.

"Yes," said Captain Fisher, "they are."

"That's impossible," said Mike. "Nobody could buy this claptrap as more than an evening's entertainment."

"Look at their faces, Mike," said Jenny. "Everything from joy to greed to astonishment. No one's laughing."

Mike and the captain kept glancing toward the faces crowded into the dim Oriental Room. The babble of voices rose, for just at that moment the dimness turned pitch black.

"Light trouble," said the voice of Rolf Wind. "Sorry."

After a few minutes, the soft lights went on again. But where Jenny Dean had been standing was a vacant spot.

"Could she have needed a breath of air?" said Captain Fisher.

"Without a word?" said Mike.

They both knew better. They left the robot prophet and the oriental mysteries of Rolf Wind's computer to start searching for their missing Jenny.

By then, Jenny was several miles away, captive in a speeding car.

CHAPTER 11

Kidnapped

The second the lights went out in the Oriental Room, a hand went over Jenny's mouth and a pointed knife touched her ribs simultaneously. Jenny had been in too many dangerous situations since she'd been working with the captain. She knew when someone threatened pain. She did not cry out, knowing intuitively that whoever held the knife wouldn't hesitate for a moment to use it. A few seconds more, and she was outside. Two men were involved at this point. They had covered her eyes so she couldn't see them. Then they put a burlap sack over her head and shoulders and quickly thrust her into a waiting car.

Jenny's sense of direction was good. Minutes later, feeling the turns of the car, she knew they were traveling north of town along Old Road, past the Springer Farm toward the old, abandoned power plant. She could be dropped down one of those old shafts and never be heard from again.

"I have to throw up," said Jenny.

"We're not stopping," said a male voice that sounded much like Rolf Wind's resonant tones.

"All over the car or not makes no difference to me," said Jenny.

"You're not getting out of the car," said the same voice.

"Whatever you say," agreed Jenny. "Any second now."

The car screeched to a halt.

"Take her over to those bushes," said the Rolf Wind voice. "And keep an eye on her."

The other man half-helped, half-pulled Jenny from the car. He led her to the bushes.

"I'm going to smell some, if I have to do it inside this bag," said Jenny, keeping her voice as calmly practical as if they were sharing arrangements for a picnic.

The man untied the rope that held the bag around Jenny's shoulders. When he pulled the burlap over her head, Jenny saw that the man was Mario.

"Orders," said Mario. "I'm sorry, young lady."

Mario may have been a frightened toady, but he was no killer.

"Mario," said Jenny. "Now is the moment. Please turn around."

"I'm not supposed to take my eyes off you for a second," said Mario.

"You aren't *seriously* going to *stand* there and *watch* me throw *up*, are you?" said Jenny.

Even someone as generally in command of herself as Jenny could sound like a silly, hysterical innocent when she wanted to. "Mario you *wouldn't*, would you!"

"All right," Mario whispered, "but make it quick."

Jenny certainly did that. The minute Mario's back was turned, Jenny was off through the darkness of the Springer Farm like Br'er Rabbit in the Briar Patch. She knew every inch of the place. The men chasing her just bumped into trees.

She was safely inside a hayloft, listening to the men cursing below. She even caught a glimpse of the other man, who looked enough like Rolf Wind to be his younger brother. Of course Mr. Wind had arranged all this.

Why?

"We better get back to work," said Rolf Wind's brother. "We've got a lot ahead of us. We've got her treed here, anyway. She won't interfere."

With what? Jenny wondered.

Jenny stayed put until she heard the car start up and take off. Why was it going northeast toward Dodgetown? Did the Wind brothers operate something new there that Jenny hadn't heard of?

Jenny used the Springer telephone to dial the captain's special number. It would either be picked up in his car, at home, or his office, or else beep his transceiver until he got to a phone to dial his answering machine.

"Captain Fisher here," came the comforting sound.

"I'm all right," said Jenny. "I'm out at the Springer Farm."

"I'll come for you, don't move. Mike's with me," said Captain Fisher.

The police car roared up the private road to the Springer's front door. Jenny piled in, told her story, and said, "Please, Captain, fast, to Ama Dablam. Those men weren't going to Dodgetown. They were going to the lamasery. I have a bad feeling in my middle about what the rest of their night's work is all about."

Jenny's feeling was entirely accurate. When they got to the lamasery, Padme Lampo was gone.

"Look what they left in his place, trying to fool

us, trying to gain a couple of hours by making us feel he was still sitting in the temple,'' said a shaking, enraged Sonam.

Jenny had the distinct sensation Sonam's protective tiger rage could turn murderous with this kind of provocation. At the moment, she shared his attitude, if not his range of solutions.

She, Mike, and the captain looked at the lotus throne where Padme Lampo had been sitting in his evening meditation. Caro kept touching what sat on the throne with grief and shock.

In place of the loving young lama, was another of Mario's well-dressed perfect duplicates, a second Padme Lampo doll like the first in Rolf Wind's Oriental Room.

Even the Siamese kitten was crying.

CHAPTER 12

The Real Thing

Sonam's dark, red-robed figure came forward to speak to Jenny. This dark silent monk had endured years of hardship and discipline in lamaseries that hung from the high snowy cliffs of mountain passes. Even the caravans of Sherpa porters rarely dared to climb them. This dark, silent monk loved his young charge enough to have come all the way from Tibet to care for and protect him.

"I can bear much," said Sonam. "But I cannot bear that something should happen to the young Grand Lama."

"We'll find him, don't worry, Sonam," said Jenny. "We know who's responsible for his kidnapping."

"Are you certain I had not better return home to consult an oracle?" said Sonam. "I mean no ordinary astrologer or soothsayer, I mean a true oracle of

the Potala, the palace at Lhasa, our capitol. I am
prepared to make the journey instantly.''

Jenny placed what she hoped was a reassuring
hand on the monk's strong arm. ''We know just
where to find Padme Lampo,'' said Jenny.

''And just where is that?'' the captain wanted to
know as they left the grounds of Ama Dablam and
were out of earshot of either Caro or Sonam.

''Mr. Rolf Wind has got Padme Lampo. Mr.
Wind has taken him away. And I know why, too. He
wants to use Padme's prophetic ability to make
more money,'' said Jenny.

''Not what the Buddha would call right action,''
said Mike.

''No, blast the hustler,'' said Jenny.

''And that's not what the Buddha would call right
speech,'' said Mike. He was trying to calm Jenny's
gathering rage.

''No good, Mike,'' said the captain. ''She's angry. Can't blame her, though. Come on, you two.
Back to town.''

Captain Fisher climbed into the police car. Jenny
and Mike climbed in after him.

''Can you bring Mr. Wind in for questioning?''
Jenny asked.

''No, but we can hang your attempted kidnapping

on his brother and Mario, who may very well admit Mr. Rolf Wind was behind *that*. Then we can bring him in, Jenny," said Captain Fisher. "And, naturally, I'll put out an All Points Bulletin and start investigating Padme Lampo's disappearance."

Mike could read Jenny's face in the dark. Proper proceedings were once again too slow for her.

"Okay," said Jenny, too agreeably too quickly.

Where is he, she sat asking herself as the car sped back to downtown Winter Falls. Where would that Rolf Wind take him?

That second robot was really exquisite, she had to admit. Mario and Rolf Wind were superb designers and technicians. Second robot? Was that *really* a second robot?

"Captain, could you take me back to the Electronic Arcade?" said Jenny. "And Captain, dear Captain, could you hurry?" She suddenly had a pretty good idea where Rolf Wind had taken Padme Lampo.

Mike read Jenny's face again. "Meeting violence with violence never ends violence. Finding another path of resistance to meet violence would change world history," said Mike in a sonorous voice.

"Who said that?" said Jenny, her rage still growing. "Buddha? Ghandi? Krishnaji?"

"There's only me and the captain in this car, Jen. You'll have to make your choice accordingly," said Mike. "One from Column A—"

He was trying to tease her out of her fury. Not only was anger uncomfortable for Jenny, Mike knew, but it tended to unbalance her judgment.

"Have calm and logic returned to our fair lady?" said Captain Fisher, as he pulled the police car to the curb in front of the Electronic Arcade.

"I'll calm logic that Rolf Wind with a cleaver," said Jenny. "No, I won't. Don't worry. I've been deep breathing the way we learned in yoga class. It sends a lot of fresh oxygen to the brain. Gives you energy, too. I'm fine, now. Really."

Jenny was out of the captain's car like a shot. She wanted no more cross-examination, no more calming down, and no more jokes.

"I'll get him," she muttered under her breath. "How dare he lay hands on that sweet, gentle soul!"

It was two hours since she had been kidnapped from the Oriental Room. Now she was back. More people continued to come into the room. Jenny pushed, crawled, and scrambled into a position forward and slightly to the side, where she could have a full view of both the computer and the robot figure of Padme Lampo. She stayed in the shadows, not wanting to call attention to any more possible kidnappers in Rolf Wind's employ.

Yet somehow, she had to make a signal. As she thought about how to go about signaling, she read on the computer screen, "Shall I invest in stocks or bonds right now in the Wall Street market?"

When there was no answer forthcoming to that question, Jenny thought even harder about signaling. Her hunch was more plausible than ever, about where Rolf Wind had hidden the kidnapped Grand Lama. In one moment more, Jenny was sure.

In a movement so rapid one had to be prepared ahead of time to know what was happening, the robot figure on the fake lotus throne opened a Third Eye in the middle of its forehead. With a quick, red, glowing flash of its ruby center, the head turned quickly toward Jenny and—winked!

Of course! Padme Lampo was a telepath! He had read Jenny's mind, heard her message, and let her know she was right.

There had been no second robot left at Ama Dablam while the real Padme Lampo was hidden away somewhere. Rolf Wind had simply arranged to have the original robot and the real Padme Lampo switched. He was here, in this fake room so like his own temple. And Rolf Wind was going to use the lama's healing and saving powers to make money only for himself.

CHAPTER 13

On Her Own

Jenny winked back. Then she formed a series of thoughts as clearly as she could, and hoped Padme Lampo was reading them.

Don't worry, we'll get you out of here, she telegraphed mentally. *Don't know how yet, but no Rolf Wind in this world or the next gets to take advantage of you, dear friend.*

Jenny wondered briefly why Padme Lampo didn't simply step down and reveal the treachery of Rolf Wind. Why did he continue to sit on the fake lotus throne, answering what questions he could answer with honesty and integrity, and avoiding questions about material gains?

There had to be a reason why he didn't try to save himself. Jenny wasn't going to find out what that reason was while she was just standing there, either.

She searched the crowds for Mike and the captain. She saw both of them against the far wall of carved arches and fresco paintings of bodhisattvas. Ordinarily, Jenny would have run and asked them to help free Padme Lampo instantly. She would have shared her discovery that it was not a robot on that throne but indeed it was the young lama himself.

But if Padme Lampo hadn't disclosed himself publicly, and only privately winked at her, he had to have a reason. Until Jenny figured out what it was, she decided that Padme Lampo wanted to remain where he was and that she had better honor his wishes for now.

As she squirmed through the awed and whispering crowds, each of whom had paid Rolf Wind five dollars for the privilege of being there, Jenny decided what she would and wouldn't do.

What she wouldn't do was admit to a thing right now.

What she would do was return later, much later, and find a way to get into the Electronic Arcade to talk to Padme Lampo.

"Thanks," said Jenny. "Thanks for bringing me. Just wanted another look at that robot to see if it matched the one at Ama Dablam."

"We can go now?" said Mike.

"I've called in an APB on the car radio, but I would like to get back to the station and back up the search," said Captain Fisher.

Jenny felt a little guilty that the captain was going to all the trouble of setting up a full-scale search. But she didn't feel guilty enough to betray Padme Lampo. She would just have to explain it all to Captain Fisher later.

"We'll be in touch. Call if you need us," said Mike.

"Where will you guys be?" said the captain.

"At Laurie Harper's house, if that's all right with Mike," said Jenny. "She's having some people over tonight. It's only going on ten o'clock. What do you say, Mike?"

"Fine with me."

"I'll drive you out there, shall I?" offered the captain.

Laurie and Joe were delighted to see them when they arrived. Jenny and Mike shared all the latest details about Jenny's brief kidnapping and Padme Lampo's more serious disappearance.

"He'll be found, Jenny," said Laurie sympathetically. She knew how attached Jenny had become to their new friend from Tibet.

Jenny entered the huge hall of the Harper mansion, where all their friends from high school were either eating from the long buffet table or dancing under the dimmed crystal chandelier.

"And they're doing those things all dressed up in their best *clothes*," Jenny remarked half out loud to herself, "while I personally have come straight, as it were, from the barnyard this morning."

It was true, she and Mike hadn't stopped all day. There had been no time to change in between veterinary rounds, the Electronic Arcade, her own kidnapping, and Padme Lampo's.

"Come on upstairs," said Laurie generously. 'Pick anything at all out of my closet."

'You go along and tend to your guests. I'll take Jenny upstairs." It was old Emily Jones, who had kept house for Laurie and her father ever since the death of Laurie's mother years before.

Part of Jenny's fuss was planned. It was perfectly true she looked a bit out of place at Laurie's party. It was also perfectly true it didn't bother her at all.

What Jenny did need, however, was a darker jacket and a dark scarf for her blond hair. She had no intention of remaining at the party for more than two hours, at which point it was curfew for all estab-

lishments that served even beer in Winter Falls. Rolf Wind's place would also close and Jenny planned to be back there exactly at closing time.

Half an hour later, Jenny came downstairs. She had showered and changed into a white silk shirt. Over her arm, however, was a black pea jacket and scarf, which she left casually over the back of a hall chair.

Claire Richmond and Alex Harte danced to a standstill. Jason Kent came over with Laurie, and Karen Porter and Joe Scott waved from across the floor.

"It's so good to see you all," said Jenny, feeling grateful that she had friends who noticed and cared about her comings and goings.

She exchanged several happy hugs. "Ah," she sighed. "Feels like a shot of vitamins."

"You know, Jenny dear," said Laurie, who put her arm around Jenny, "you don't have to live in this half-starved condition of yours. If you spent half the time with us that you spend saving everybody and everything from disaster, you wouldn't look half-crazed half the time."

"I'm half-numb from this hug, too," said Jenny, "and half-hungry and half-thirsty and half-ready to dance."

"If you want me, I'm half-asleep in this corner," said Mike. He had literally propped himself up against the wall. "Some of us who were up milking at five this morning and haven't stopped since are about ready to drop."

"Drop," said Jenny, laughing at the sight of him edging toward her along the wall. "Just drop there, and we'll bring you food."

Jenny was encouraging everybody's humor so that when she slipped away in an hour, she would leave behind enough images of herself to suggest she was really part of the party. That way they wouldn't miss her.

At eleven-thirty, Jenny made certain she was in the middle of a lighted and laughing circle of friends. At eleven-thirty-five, she had slipped away from the Harper mansion with the black jacket and scarf. She headed quickly over to Willow Street and to her own home. She didn't go inside. She got her bike from the garage, wheeled it quietly out to the street, and took off like a shot for downtown Winter Falls.

The alley between the Orpheum Movie Theater and the Electronic Arcade was dark. Most of the lights had been shut off. The crowds had gone home.

From the shadows, Jenny heard Mr. Wind saying goodnight to the last of his customers, receiving their congratulations for adding not only to their entertainment, but also to the well-being of Winter Falls.

"I feel the fortune-teller will really bring us good fortune," Jenny heard someone's greedy voice say.

"Phooey," said Jenny into the darkness, "on you all."

She had to make three leaps before she managed to grab the lowest rung of the fire-escape ladder Mike had helped her with the night before. But she made it up to the fire escape and to the window that overlooked the Oriental Room.

One push, and two of the crusted glass panes dropped out of the old window. Jenny reached in and opened the window which was wide enough to let her slip through and drop to the floor.

Though it was dim inside, she could see, however, that the lotus throne was vacant.

What had they done with Padme Lampo now?

CHAPTER 14

Circus Companions

Like the quiet, deserted streets, lit only by pale streetlights, this empty, deserted chamber was lit by only a few flickering butter lamps. Jenny felt the silence deeply. It wasn't a peaceful stillness at all. It had foreboding in it.

Where was Padme Lampo?

A figure moved in the shadows behind the lotus throne.

"Who's there?" it said.

Jenny froze in her tracks. Then she recognized the voice.

"Padme Lampo!" she said. "You're all right? You aren't locked up in a closet. Why haven't you tried to escape? Never mind. I'm here now. I'll get you out of here. Wish I'd asked Mike to come now. Or at least telephoned the captain to bring a rope or something. We're going to have a problem getting us both up through that window. Come on, you first. No time to lose."

While Jenny was chattering nervously and eyeing the window, measuring her ability to hoist the young lama onto her shoulders and out through the narrow opening, Padme Lampo was just standing there.

"You're just standing there," Jenny finally noticed. "Come on. And watch out for that can of open paint." Mario must still be working on finishing touches. "Why, oh why, didn't I bring Mike? I mean, I somehow felt this was your secret and I ought not to betray it, that's why, but I still wish he was here."

"I put as strong a message into your mind as I could, considering you're not telepathic," said Padme Lampo. "I hope I haven't endangered your life by asking you to come alone, but you see, you didn't bring help because I asked you not to. You see, dear Jenny—I don't want to be rescued. Please now, go back and tell the others not to try."

"Why?" said Jenny. "What are they holding over you, Padme Lampo?"

"Ah, you do understand," said the young lama.

"I understand," said Jenny. "What are they holding over you?"

"Caro," said Padme Lampo. "They said they would hurt Caro."

"Trouble," muttered Jenny. "That madman is nothing but trouble." Then she added, "But if you can mind control my behavior, why can't you plant a message in Rolf Wind's mind to let go of Caro and you and me and all of this?" Jenny waved her arm to include the whole Oriental Room fraud.

Padme Lampo's laughter was like silver bells.

"But I can't mind control," he said. "I can only help by making telepathic suggestions to those people who have healthy and willing minds to begin with."

"Well," said Jenny. "I'm certainly willing. What do you want to do? What do you want *me* to do?"

A gust of wintry night air and Rolf Wind's sudden entrance put an end to the conversation and the decision-making. He had a decision of his own to announce.

"It's too dangerous for me to keep you here, Mr. Lampo, *sir*," the deep, resonant voice said mockingly. "I have therefore decided to send you and your throne and your lamps, and all these trappings of Mario's, to a friend of mine. My friend manages a sideshow in a traveling circus. He thinks you will make quite a money-making concession for us all. Also, because you will be traveling around, you can be easily hidden from friends who decide to search for you.''

Mr. Wind made a mocking bow toward Jenny.

"As for your annoying friend—"

"You kidnapped me so I wouldn't guess at or interfere with your switching the robot for Padme Lampo, right?" said Jenny.

"That's right," said Rolf Wind.

"And then I'll bet you were responsible for the slight problem with the lights an hour and a half later, too. That's when you made the switch, right?" said Jenny.

"That's right," said Rolf Wind. "But how did you know for sure that I had made the switch when you came back earlier this evening?"

"For one thing, Padme Lampo wouldn't answer questions about money and business," said Jenny. "His powers aren't to be used for gain."

"A matter of time," said Rolf Wind, "until we *convince* him. But was that all? Was there no flaw, no slight difference that told you? I want to know so Mario can make corrections in any future robots. The real Padme Lampo knows more than any robot and we will therefore make far more money from him. But if something should happen—well, we'll just make a better robot next time, that's all. Now tell me, was there any other small difference you noticed?''

Jenny had no intention of revealing the truth about Padme Lampo's Third Eye.

"No matter for now," said Rolf Wind, "since you are going to accompany your friend to the traveling circus. We will have many opportunities for further chats."

Rolf Wind was right for the moment. Padme Lampo would not do anything about his own life until Caro was safe. And Jenny Dean would not do anything about her own safety until Padme Lampo was safe. Since she couldn't rescue them both right now under Rolf Wind's nose, Jenny went along quietly. The car was waiting.

"No need to blindfold you," said Rolf Wind. He put Padme Lampo and Jenny in the back seat. He got into the front seat next to his brother who drove, and turned to keep an eye on his prisoners. "As soon as we get to the circus, the performers will be leaving for their next stop anyway. Who knows where you will be going? Not a bad way to see the world, really. You'll get to travel, we'll all make some money, and none of us will ever have to see hum-drum old Winter Falls again soon."

"I happen to love humdrum old Winter Falls," said Jenny, feeling it was the only response she could safely make.

The car started and they were off, heading north.

Mike Ward and Captain Fisher had guessed by then where Jenny had gone and, pulling up outside the Electronic Arcade, had missed them by ten minutes.

By three o'clock the following Sunday morning, everybody was pale with exhaustion. The truck driver, who together with Mario had dismantled and packed up the entire contents of the Oriental Room, had arrived to set the whole thing up again in a readied circus wagon.

Padme Lampo had posed, pretending to be his own duplicated robot, for publicity pictures which were to be circulated during the succeeding days of travel and performance.

Jenny, needing no ropes and gags because Rolf Wind knew she wouldn't desert Padme Lampo, eyed and circled the whole operation like a tigress with a treed cub.

At four o'clock in the morning, Operation Padme Lampo was complete. To a cry of "Roll 'em," the small, traveling circus wagon train took off up the road. And inside one of the wagons, between two elephants in the wagon in front of them, and the Fat Lady and her Tattooed Husband in the wagon behind, The Magical Computerized Fortune-Teller and his friend, Jenny Dean, rode the open highways with *Tonio's Traveling Circus*.

Jenny wondered if this time, she'd gone too far out on a limb to ever get back. The list of missing persons who were never found was longer than most of the public generally realized.

CHAPTER 15

The Third-Eye Rescue

All Sunday, the roustabouts worked.

That night, in a small town in northwestern Kansas Jenny hadn't yet spotted the name of, *Tonio's Traveling Circus*, including its new sideshow attraction, The Magical Fortune-Teller from the Mysterious Orient, gave a full performance.

Tonio himself was his own barker. He dressed in top hat, white riding pants and black boots, and the traditional red-tailed jacket of the ringmaster. His call rang out in front of his beautiful red-and-white-striped, big-top circus tent.

"Come one, come all, we welcome children of all ages," called Tonio. "Before the main show in the big tent, see all the miracles of our sideshow. See the Fat Lady and her Tattooed Husband. See the Snake-Charmer, the Bearded Girl, the Frog Person. And most of all, see the newest addition to *Tonio's*

Traveling Circus, the Magical Fortune-Teller from the Mysterious Orient. He will answer any and all questions you may have about your futures, your love life, your money, anything at all, any question at all.''

Jenny, idiotically dressed in a harem costume, stood beside Padme Lampo. He was a huge success. He didn't answer one question about material gain. Instead he told people about their health—how herbs and physical exercise can help cure them. Each questioner went away confused, but apparently pleased.

"You don't look so happy," said Padme Lampo in a hushed whisper to Jenny. "Don't worry. We'll think of some way to get you out of this. Caro isn't your problem, she's my friend."

"Don't *you* worry," said Jenny, frowning. "I've already thought of a way to get us all out of this, I hope! I'm just waiting for it to happen."

What Jenny was waiting for might take some time. She only hoped that the clue she had managed to leave for Mike and the captain had been found.

It hadn't yet.

Captain Fisher and Mike Ward surveyed the Oriental Room at the back of the Electronic Arcade

in dismay. No Rolf Wind, no Mario. Worst of all, no Padme Lampo and no Jenny Dean.

The captain again headed outside to his police car parked at the curb.

"Any word on Padme Lampo?" He spoke into the microphone of his car radio. "Because now Jenny Dean's gone, too."

Sergeant Kirk answered from the police station.

"None, Captain. We've got out an All Points Bulletin, we've got checkpoints on the highways, the toll booths have been notified, the whole works," said the sergeant. "I'll provide a description of Jenny Dean now, too."

"Good," said the captain. "Stay close."

"Right, sir," said Sergeant Kirk. "Nothing at your end? Nothing at the Electronic Arcade?" The sergeant paused. "That young friend of yours, Jenny, is a smart girl. If she were taken from there, she may have left something."

Mike Ward, who had stayed behind searching the Oriental Room, rushed out of the building just then. He spoke a few words to the captain, who then relayed the information to Sergeant Kirk.

Then Captain Fisher said, "Sergeant, I want you to track down every traveling carnival, circus and gypsy caravan in Kansas. They must all have licenses, so check them out. Have every man at the station get on the phone. Make calls all over the state. I want the exact location of every circus in Kansas. As soon as it's light, get the choppers going.''

The captain clapped Mike on the back. "Good work," he said. "That's a good clue. That Jenny is incredible to have thought of that. Let's go.''

The two climbed into the police car. Rarely did the captain use his siren. Tonight, he clapped the flashing red light on the car's roof and turned the siren up.

Sergeant Kirk radioed that the nearest of the traveling circuses was heading south.

The captain and Mike caught up with their first circus about three o'clock Sunday morning. The fat, old circus owner appeared at the door of his trailer in a flapping nightshirt.

''Have you got a search warrant?'' he demanded, after the captain explained the purpose of their sudden visit.

''If you insist I get one and waste the time doing it,'' said the captain, ''I can assure you the search will be a lot messier. I'm looking for a *friend*. I don't even accuse you of harboring her.''

''Well, I thank you for that,'' said the owner

dryly. "Do come on, then. We've got two shows tomorrow—today, that is."

The search took time. But it was fruitless.

"Not a sign of them," said Mike.

"Don't look so haunted. We'll find them," said the captain. "We'll find Jenny, Mike," he added gently.

By now it was four-thirty in the morning. The longer they took to find Jenny, the more time Tonio's circus troupe would have to get farther away.

"Dead end," radioed the captain.

"Nothing here yet," Sergeant Kirk radioed back. "There are traveling circuses stopped outside of Salina. No news—not even a rumor did we pick up—none of these hustlers would tell on another."

"Now, don't jump to conclusions, Sergeant," said the captain, who chided anyone for any generalization whatever. "Which circus is nearest Mike and me right now?"

"A caravan with a sideshow, animals, and a small tent is headed due west, about ninety miles," said Sergeant Kirk, adding the approximate travel time and the place where the caravan was last seen.

Keeping siren and flashing light going, Captain Fisher gunned the car to its limit. They made the ninety miles in an hour.

By six o'clock Sunday morning, it was clear that

Jenny Dean and Padme Lampo were not with that caravan.

By eight o'clock Sunday night, they had searched one more circus, and two small, traveling carnivals that had mostly games, dancing girls, and magicians.

Grimly, the captain and Mike Ward sped on, covering most of south, and then west Kansas. Other patrol cars sped to other parts of the state.

So far, no one had found, heard of, knew anything about Rolf Wind, his brother, a designer named Mario—or their captives.

Meanwhile, half-way through Sunday evening's first performance, Jenny and Padme Lampo began experiencing tension from the audience.

"Listen, weird person or whatever you are, I asked about which horses I should play tomorrow, not about the pain in my lower back," shouted the latest questioner in the audience.

"Yeah," shouted another customer, sounding even more outraged than his neighbor. "How about answering the questions we ask, instead of telling us who has a headache and how to make it better? Now, I want to know about my store. Will I make more money by keeping it or by selling it?"

Jenny watched Padme Lampo to see if he was getting upset. Something in the young man's training must have prepared him for anything. He sat there as serenely as if they were flattering, instead of insulting him. And the insults began to get worse.

"Hey, you mind-reading freak, you're probably just full of bull, anyway."

"No, he isn't," shouted a defender. "He was absolutely right about the weakness in my daughter's legs. I'm grateful for what he told me. What's more important, health or money, anyway?"

"If you mean *my* money, or *your* health, I can tell you right off—*my* money," came the raucous answer.

Then they started in on Jenny.

"What do you suppose the girl is for?" yelled the voice of a man who sounded drunk, Jenny thought.

Another drunk shrieked his appreciation for the crude humor. Then he pushed his way to the front of the crowd, and began to climb onto Padme Lampo and Jenny's circus wagon. He was large and heavy. He smelled of whiskey. The whites of his little cruel eyes were reddened with booze and the unspent rage of a lifetime. Jenny knew instantly this was no nightclub rowdy.

He was so quick, she had no time to move away.

Not that she would have left Padme Lampo's side, but she might have found a weapon, something to use to drive him back. But there wasn't time, and Jenny froze helplessly in front of Padme Lampo, trying to protect him as much as she could.

Only it wasn't the young lama the man wanted to hurt. He balanced himself and then lurched, grabbing for the pretty young girl in the harem pants.

Jenny felt his suffocating chest against her face and smelled his revolting breath. Then just as the drunk grabbed Jenny, she felt a force quickly thrust her away from his grasp.

The drunk screamed in fright. As he screamed, and as Jenny fell from him, the audience gasped so loudly it sounded like rolling ocean waves.

Jenny turned to Padme Lampo for a clue as to what was going on. Why had the man dropped her the minute he picked her up? Why had he screamed? What was the matter with the audience?

The minute Jenny looked at Padme Lampo, she knew the answer. There sat her friend, the young Grand Lama, trained in the most serious and necessary arts of the future world, able with his powers to heal throngs, read the minds and hearts of whole cities, and change lives in both obvious and subtle ways. There he sat, dignified, calm, and gentle as always—and winking at the evil drunk with his Third Eye. That eye, to Jenny now an understood and accepted part of her friend, was so bizarre both to the drunk and the crowd, that it set them all back on their heels.

No one was going to mess with a creature—robot or not—who could open a Third Eye and who could cast a dark, ruby-red gleam at them from the middle of his forehead.

"I thought you were supposed to only use that for some ultimate good," Jenny whispered.

"I used it for an ultimate good," said Padme Lampo. "I used it to save you. I had to scare that horrible man away from you."

It was even weirder now, when Padme Lampo went back to his more mechanical behavior for the next two or three questions. The crowd stopped taunting for a few minutes, no longer sure whether they were addressing a man or a machine.

"Either way, it's freaky," stage-whispered an old woman, "he's just too right-on about whatever he says, that fortune-teller, man *or* computer."

Thinking about Rolf Wind's intentions, the whole business of being kidnapped, and the trickiness of dealing with the crowds, Jenny was growing more frightened. She put her hand on Padme Lampo's shoulder for comfort and to comfort. Where was help? With the growing darkness, she was feeling whatever hope she had had was falling away into the night.

CHAPTER 16

Just Desserts

A few seconds later, police car sirens brought this particular Sunday night circus performance, somewhere in the northwest of Kansas, to an end.

"Caro!" Padme Lampo cried out, standing up from his fake lotus throne, all pretense at being a mechanical robot gone.

Sergeant Kirk and his men had brought Caro, too worried to remain behind, on this final search into the northwest mountains. Overcome with relief and affection, she ran to hug, rather than bow to, her dear old friend.

"Hey, he's no computer after all," shouted someone in the crowd. "This whole thing's a fraud. How do we know this guy's telling us the truth? A machine is something you can trust, but a *person*?"

"That speaks well for the modern world," Jenny giggled. She was so relieved that they had found the clue she had left.

"And just what do you think you're wearing?" said Captain Fisher, his stuffy reaction to her brief pink top, bare midriff, and see-through billowing white harem pants, didn't surprise her.

"I think she looks cute," said Mike. He lifted her down from the circus wagon and put his coat around her. "For my eyes only, however," Mike added.

While the police were rounding up Rolf Wind, his brother, Nelson, Mario, and Tonio for questioning, the captain complimented Jenny.

"Good, fast thinking, Jenny. I do wish you'd play things a little less smart and a little more safe," said the captain.

"It really wasn't such a complicated plan to deserve such a compliment," said Jenny. "It was just all I could think of at the time."

Very simply, back when Rolf Wind had made his long-winded speech to her and Padme Lampo about his clever plan to have them travel with the circus, Jenny had used her boot toe to write "FIND CIRCUS"—by dipping her boot over and over again into the can of black paint that Mario had left.

"I couldn't get away from Rolf Wind to phone much less run away to get help. If I had, he'd have fulfilled his promise to hurt Caro without a second thought. But as long as he felt Padme Lampo and I were hostages without much hope of being found, all of us were safe," Jenny explained. "It was a long shot, leaving only that message for you," she apologized, knowing how worried they must have been. "But truly, there was nothing else I could think of doing without endangering *somebody*, Caro, Padme Lampo, somebody."

Now a caravan was going in the other direction. It was a caravan of police cars heading back to Winter Falls, with Tonio, Rolf and Nelson Wind, and Mario in the first two cars. Jenny and Mike rode in the third car with the captain.

By midnight, all had been settled.

"Are you certain you won't press charges, Padme Lampo?" asked Captain Fisher. "You have every right to charge Rolf Wind and his friends with everything from kidnapping to fraud."

Padme Lampo smiled. "With Jenny's permission, because she and everyone else also suffered from all this. I think there is more justice in accepting Mr. Tonio's offer."

Rolf Wind paled visibly.

Tonio had backed Rolf Wind's enterprises so far. Tonio had originally laid out the money for the Electronic Arcade; he had also laid out the money for the Oriental Room, and he had even paid for transporting everything to his circus. Every time his old circus friend, Rolf Wind, came up with a good idea, Tonio had agreed to be a business partner.

"However," Tonio had said angrily, "Rolf never told me about kidnapping or stealing rooms from other people's temples. He never said a word about that. I'm very angry and very upset. For this, he must pay me back. He is a good barker. He can be my circus barker and work for me for the next ten years. And I can assure you, for acting so badly to such good people, Rolf will work hard."

"How can we be sure he won't run off?" said Mike. Mike had no sense of revenge. But this was one time, Padme Lampo being such a gentle soul, even Mike wanted to see justice done.

Tonio stood six-and-a-half feet tall, with the breadth and muscle of two men. His smile under the bristling black moustache was positively horrrible.

"Run away from me?" Tonio roared throughout the police station. "Rolf should just try! I'll also take Mario and young Nelson with me to work for good measure. That will give me three extra hands, and Winter Falls will be rid of all of them."

"Sounds fine to me," said Padme Lampo. "But Jenny must also agree."

Jenny liked the looks of Tonio. He would be as good as his word. She nodded her agreement.

"What about the Electronic Arcade?" she asked.

"I'll take it back into my ownership in payment for what Rolf Wind still owes me," said Tonio. "And I'll leave it to you, who know the people of this town, to pick a manager to run the arcade."

Back at the Ama Dablam lamasery, behind the quiet walls and under the gentle curved roofs and overhanging boughs of the old oak and elm trees, Sonam and Caro hosted one of the best dinners Jenny and Mike had ever had. Jenny's parents along with Jack Ward and Mike's brother, George, had been invited, as well as Captain Fisher, Laurie Harper, and Joe Scott. They celebrated Jenny and the lama's safe return. And they looked forward to the good work of Padme Lampo, Caro, and Sonam in Winter Falls.

The dinner was served, not in the Great Hall— they had all had enough of lotus thrones and carved arcades and butter lamps for a while—but upstairs in Padme Lampo's private apartment. They sat on lovely rugs and leaned on huge, soft floor cushions. In front of each were small tables filled with endless dishes from the kitchen below.

"Do you think, Jenny and Mike," Dr. Howard began, "and I'm sure I speak for all friends and relatives concerned, that we might look forward to a

week or two of peace and quiet before something else, whatever it may be, happens?''

Dr. Gwen hugged her daughter and smiled. ''Whatever happens, always seems to happen to Jenny, doesn't it?''

''And to me, too,'' said Mike.

''A rest wouldn't hurt, though,'' said Joe, who was thoroughly enjoying both Caro's food and her company. They were comparing shiatsu with acupuncture as muscle relaxers.

''I promise,'' the captain said, ''not to tempt Jenny nor be tempted by her into any case for a while unless it involves something as serious, say, as a mystery from outer space.''

''Funny you should say that, Captain,'' said Jenny, diverting attention from her plate for the first time in half an hour. ''I'm going to visit a cousin of mine during the Thanksgiving holiday. She lives in the middle of cyclone country on the open Kansas plains. I've always wondered if Oz could have actually been an invisible city from outer space, hidden in the eye of that cyclone—''

''She's off again,'' Mike said, and Jenny heard Padme Lampo and Caro laugh along with the others.

But Jenny's instincts and intuitions often had a truth of their own. Thanksgiving was coming soon, and with it, *The Secret of the Invisible City*.

About the Author

Dale Carlson is the author of over thirty books for young people. Three of them, *The Mountain of Truth*, *The Human Apes*, and *Girls Are Equal Too* were ALA Notable Books; and her *Where's Your Head?* won a Christopher Award.

Ms. Carlson says that her daughter Hannah, "edits all my current books, and also provides my favorite heroines. She is particularly the heroine of *The Jenny Dean Science Fiction Mysteries*." Her son Danny, coauthored her book *The Shining Pool*.

Ms. Carlson lives in New York City.

WIN JENNY DEAN'S BIKE!

You can win a super 15-speed bike—just like the one that Jenny Dean rides! Guaranteed quality from a leading American manufacturer, fully warranted. All you have to do is fill out your name and address on the coupon below, clip, and send to:

**"Win Jenny Dean's Bike" Contest, Dept. 3,
Marketing Department,
Putnam Publishing Group,
51 Madison Avenue, New York, N.Y. 10010**

All entries must be received by March 30, 1984

Contest Rules: All entries must be received at above address by close of business on Friday, March 30, 1984. Winner will be selected at random. No purchase necessary. (Alternate means of entry: send information below on a postcard to "Win Jenny Dean's Bike" Contest.) Employees of MCA, Inc., including subsidiaries and affiliates, and their families, are ineligible to be contestants. Contest void where prohibited by law. All federal, state and local regulations apply. Contestants must reside in U.S.A.

✂ *cut here*

Yes, please enter me for the *free* "Win Jenny Dean's Bike" contest.

NAME _____

ADDRESS _____

CITY _____ STATE_____ ZIP_____

AGE_____ HEIGHT_____

Clip and send in this coupon today!
Deadline for receipt of entries: March 30, 1984

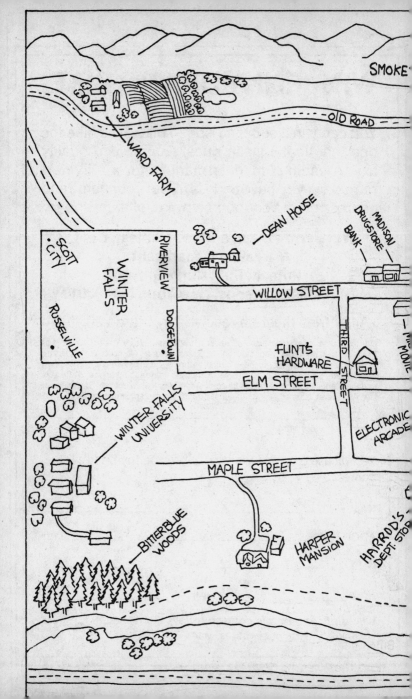